FOR A DANCER

A TOMMY SHORE MYSTERY

LAWRENCE DORFMAN

ROUGH
EDGES
PRESS

For a Dancer
Paperback Edition
Copyright © 2022 Lawrence Dorfman

Rough Edges Press
An Imprint of Wolfpack Publishing
5130 S. Fort Apache Rd. 215-380
Las Vegas, NV 89148

roughedgespress.com

Paperback ISBN 978-1-68549-132-1
eBook ISBN 978-1-68549-131-4
LCCN 2022941282

FOR A DANCER

"Down these mean streets a man must go who is not himself mean, who is neither tarnished nor afraid."
  –Raymond Chandler

ONE

She was sitting at the middle of the bar, nursing a martini with her left hand while twirling the end of her long red hair with her right, deeply lost in thought. I was sitting at the end of the bar, in the one seat that gave me a complete view of all the others. She was very attractive and I was trying to look at her covertly, glancing over every few minutes or so, trading off between where she sat and the TV screen over the bar, where the Celtics were soundly beating the Knicks.

She seemed to be talking to herself. Not in the "crazy as a loon muttering" kind of way but more in a "figuring out two sides of a dilemma, self-reviewing" sort of way. It appeared to be a long and quite involved wordless conversation. I was fascinated. I was also a little drunk.

I seemed to be the only one there interested. The guy who sat on her right hadn't looked away from the game in the last twenty minutes while the couple on her left were having barstool sex, pawing at each other within the confines of a public place while still trying to heat each other up. I figured them for another three minutes or so before they paid their tab and left to find a hotel room or a backseat somewhere. I decided that, when it happened, I would go sit next to her and start up a conversation. That was the immediate plan. It changed abruptly when I turned back to look at her and she was gone. I'd missed my moment.

I was spending a lot of time in the Owl bar. It had been four months since my last paying case of any note. I'd recently picked up a few dollars tailing a cheating husband for a divorce lawyer I knew and a few more watching a convenience store after hours when it was discovered that stuff had been routinely disappearing. The owner found my name in the local paper and didn't want to pay the prices the real pros got. It turned out to be the guy's teenage son, who was trying to win over friends at his high school by supplying beer and smokes to the cool kids. It only took two nights of watching the back door to the place to catch them in the act. I took some pictures and jotted down some notes, the license plate and descriptions. The owner paid me $500 and begged me not to say anything to anyone, that he would handle it. I said it would of course stay confidential and he threw in a case of beef jerky.

I had been getting antsy and bored of late and the bills had started piling up. Something needed to pop soon but spending time trying to find full-time work felt like a useless endeavor, especially when I could just come across the street to the Owl and drink instead.

"This seat taken?"

It took me out of my reverie. I looked up and saw it was her, the red-headed mumbler.

I smiled and swept my arm out to indicate that it

was open. She reached under the bar, placing her over-sized handbag onto one of the hooks there while smoothly sliding onto the barstool that was kitty-corner to mine.

I put out my hand. "Tommy Shore."

She looked at me a few seconds, chuckled, then shook it. "I know who you are." It took me back a little. She reached down into her bag, rummaged around, and brought out a pack of American Spirit cigarettes and a slim, gold lighter. She took one out, lit it, then turned her head slightly and blew the smoke out towards the open part of the bar. It was an elaborate routine. My first thought was that it was practiced. My second was that she was even more beautiful up close. And younger, maybe 24. I decided to play along.

"I'm flattered. How do you know me?"

She smiled. I got a feeling this was a game she liked playing.

"You're a private dick...right?"

She said it in a way that was intended to make it sound dirty, although it may have been the three Jameson's I'd already consumed that gave me that impression.

I took my time answering. "Well, I've been known to do investigative work occasionally. Are you in need of investigating?"

This conversation was going in a direction I wasn't sure I was comfortable with yet. I decided to change it.

"What's your name?"

She took another pull off her cigarette.

"Well, my stage name is Candy, but you can call me Jessika. With a *k*."

I looked into her eyes, but I couldn't tell if she was still playing or if she was telling me the truth.

"Well, Jessika with a *k*, would you like a drink? I seem to remember you were drinking red wine when you were sitting further down the bar. Can I get you another?"

She nodded and chuckled again. "Very observant of you. A girl always likes to know she's getting a man's attention."

I smiled and signaled for the bartender, Joe, to come over and pour her a new glass. He did, then walked back to the other end of the bar to give us a little privacy.

"You mentioned a stage name. Are you a performer?"

I had already guessed the answer, but it was clear that she needed to go through the motions.

"I am. I dance. At the Catwalk. I'm an exotic dancer."

I smiled again at the euphemism, like garbage men who call themselves disposal technicians. She was a stripper.

The Catwalk was a strip club that was located down on East Street and had been there forever. The sign outside said GENTLEMEN'S CLUB but there were very few gentlemen that frequented the place. It had a fair amount of notoriety and over the years had survived a number of attempts to shut it down. Drug busts, murder investigations, mob raids – the owners had beaten every rap and it was still the only after-hours club doing business in New Haven.

It was also known as a place to find sex for a price. Even their motto subtly spoke to it: "Where you don't have to look good to close the deal." Truth in advertising.

I'd been inside a few times, mostly looking for "lost" husbands and a few times as an invitee to various bachelor parties over the years. My recollection of the place was that it had an unappealing aroma of stale air, sweat, cheap cologne, and desperation. The decor was a weird amalgam of seedy disco mixed with seedy hunting lodge, with cheap wood paneling throughout. I also remembered that there were back rooms for "private dances" and that you were allowed to BYOB. It was one of the nastier places in the city.

I brought my focus back to Candy/Jessika. I realized that I hadn't responded to her telling me she was a dancer, so I tried to fake some interest.

"Huh. Sounds fun. Been at it long?"

If there had been a lameness meter nearby, the dial would have spun around several times.

She looked at me, ignored the question, and got to the point.

"I have a girlfriend who works at Diesel Bar, and she told me about you. I'd like to hire you, Tommy. May I call you Tommy?"

It was a strange question, overly proper given the place we were in. I knew who she was referring to. I'd done a job a few months back and had spoken to a waitress who worked there. She helped me with some key information.

"Of course, it being my name and all." I smiled but I could feel myself getting annoyed for no apparent reason. "So, what might you need my services for, Jess? Can I call you Jess?"

I realized as I said it that I needed to tone down the sarcasm.

I saw her wince slightly, but she recovered quickly and dropped the "come hither" tone in her voice. It was replaced with one tinged with fear.

"I have a stalker at work. It's made my life a living hell. I'm having trouble sleeping and, as a result, trouble working. I need someone to look into it, find out who the scumbag is, and convince him that he needs to stop immediately. In the strongest possible terms."

I nodded and let it hang out there. She was scared and the words had come tumbling out quickly. I didn't know it for a fact, but it certainly made perfect sense that a woman doing this type of a job would get all manner of crazy attracted to her.

"Okay, tell me the story. Nice and slow."

She lit another cigarette, this time without the ceremony. It was clear she was trying to keep it together and gather her thoughts, deciding on where to start. She took a large swig of wine. After a minute, she looked around and asked if there was some place quieter we could go. I thought for a minute and suggested that we could walk down to the lobby of the Omni Hotel on Temple Street. They had small nests of easy chairs there, far enough away from the check-in desk, where we could talk in relative privacy. It was nearby and would be a quick walk. She said okay.

I got Joe's attention and he pulled my check. I paid and we left to walk the block down to the hotel. I was feeling the effects of the drinks but was able to steady myself, thinking this might turn out to be an interesting evening after all.

TWO

We crossed College Street and headed down the alley next to my apartment building, then crossed Temple and walked into the Omni Hotel. It was cool for May and, although I was thankful to have a windbreaker on, it only took a few minutes to get to the hotel.

The Omni Hotel had been built in 1966 and immediately became a focal point of the city. There was a restaurant on the 19th floor called John Davenport's, named after one of New Haven's founding fathers some 380 years prior. The food there was just okay but the restaurant had a spectacular view of the city and the harbor and it had become very popular with the brunch crowd. I wasn't among those people.

We entered the lobby from the parking circle, through two sets of revolving doors. The lobby was expansive, dotted with pods of leather chairs and black lacquered tables throughout. It gave off the vibe of a fancy hotel, although my memories of the few times I'd stayed there before I found my apartment were very different. It was serviceable at best. But I still had the towels.

I spotted a bevy of chairs in the back of the lobby and guided her toward them, grabbing an apple out of a bowl that was sitting on one of the tables we passed. Never know how long these things might take.

Jessika was fidgety. She had been looking around constantly on the short walk down and it continued in the hotel. She was clearly spooked about something. When I pointed to the area we finally settled in, she hesitated, then chose a couch against the back wall so she could see everything. They used to call that Wyatt Earp Syndrome. You needed to have a complete view for when they came gunning for you. I'd read recently that it was now being studied as a symptom of PTSD. Seemed appropriate.

I tried to keep it light and softly asked her to continue telling me everything. I could tell she wanted a cigarette. She opened and closed her bag a few times, rummaging around, until she remembered she couldn't light up here, which was followed by a huge sigh. When she looked up at me, her eyes were moist. This was going to take a while.

"Where do I start, where to start? Well, my real name is Jessika Quinlan. Like I told you, I dance at the Catwalk. I know I called myself an exotic dancer but I'm basically a stripper. There's really nothing exotic or erotic about it." She smiled tightly as she said it. I nodded.

"I've been doing it for about three years now. I started when I was going to grad school at Quinnipiac. My student loans had come due, and it was a way that I could work nights and make a decent amount of cash. On some nights, I can clear almost a thousand dollars."

I made a mental note to raise my rates. I was clearly in the wrong profession.

She started to go on but stopped. "Don't you need to take notes?"

I smiled and tapped my temple. "All in here. Steel trap. Go on, Jennifer."

She laughed at my lame attempt at a joke, nodded and continued.

"Anyway, about three months ago, I got this package, delivered to the club but addressed to me. I opened it and inside the brown paper wrapping was a shoe box and inside the box, in tissue paper, was a Barbie Doll. The doll was naked except for a small jack knife stuck between her legs."

She had an involuntary intake of breath as she said it and started crying. I got up to grab a wad of tissues out of a box that was on a nearby table and handed them to her. She thanked me and I sat back down and waited. She went on.

"I have no idea who sent it. As you can imagine, we get more than our share of weirdos and perverts. The rule of the club is, when a patron touches one of us inappropriately, we signal the bouncers and they take care of it. But this was different. I've racked my brain trying to remember if I said something or did something to lead one of the customers on that would bring this out. I can't for the life of me remember anything like that."

She was in full sob now. I waited. Some of the nearby guests were looking over, trying to see if she needed to be saved from me. I waved at them.

After a few minutes, she had herself under control. She went into her purse again and came out with a prescription bottle. She looked up and asked me if I could get her some water.

I looked around, then got up and went over to the concierge desk. I stood in front of it for almost a minute before a security guard who had been by the door finally came over.

"Can I help you, Sir?"

I smiled and asked if anyone had a small bottle of water that I could have. He looked at me and furrowed his eyebrows.

"Are you a guest of the hotel, Sir?"

I didn't want to get into anything, so I responded, "Not yet. My fiancé and I are trying to decide if we want to have the wedding reception here. So far, things look good."

He looked over to where Jessika was. I could tell he was skeptical, but he went through a door behind the desk and came out with a tiny water bottle, which he handed to me. I nodded my thanks, said we'll share it, then walked back to where we were sitting and handed it to Jess.

"Drink slow."

She used it to swallow the pill and continued telling me what she wanted me to do.

"I want to hire you to find this guy. I need to get back my peace of mind. I can't sleep, I can't work...I'm seeing threats in everything and everybody. I'm scared, Mr. Shore, and I don't know what to do!"

She was getting hysterical again and I could see her fighting a losing battle to keep control.

I took it all in. This would be a tough case to get

into. I would need access to the club and the ability to ask a lot of questions. I was pretty sure it wouldn't go over well at that kind of place. In a perfect world, there would be surveillance tapes, but my limited knowledge of these establishments also made me think they wouldn't chance having cameras in a place where anonymity was valued or even required.

I told her my rates, $250 a day plus expenses. She looked in her purse again and came out with a wad of cash, peeling off twenty fifties. I was happy it wasn't all in singles. She put the money on the table, but I hesitated to pick it up.

"Look, before I agree to this, I have some questions. First, will the owners of the club cooperate? I'm going to need to ask a lot of questions and I'm pretty sure that can make some proprietors nervous. I'll need access."

She was nodding yes but I was still skeptical.

"Does anyone else know about the package and what was in it?"

She inhaled, then let her breath out slowly. "There was another girl in the dressing room with me, TJ, another dancer. She was there when I opened it. I asked her to keep it to herself and she said she would. We're friends and I trust her. And there's a bartender I'm close to. Victor. He knows about it and said he'd help."

I looked at her for a minute before I spoke again. I was still deciding.

"Is there an ex-lover, an ex-husband, an ex-wife, a fiancé...anything like that?"

She shook her head. "No, I don't have any time for that. I've been focused on my studies. Besides, most guys seem to have an issue with my dancing in one of those clubs."

I nodded, although I knew a few guys who would kill to date someone who danced at one of those clubs.

"Okay, I'll look into it." I reached down and picked up the money and handed half of it back to her.

She started to protest but I put my hand up for her to stop.

"Look, if I get a sense after a couple days that I can get you some answers, I'll take the rest."

I took a small pad and a pen out of my pocket and handed it to her. "Write down the names of the people you mentioned and anyone else you think might know something. When you go back, let them know I'll be around. Write down a contact number for you, too."

She jotted the names and the information on the paper quickly. I handed her my card and told her to call me whenever she wanted but that I would be in touch soon. She nodded, stood up abruptly, said "Thank you" and walked out of the lobby. Just like that. I watched her get into a cab that was waiting in front of the hotel. I hung back, ate the apple, and drank the rest of the water. When I was done, I stood up and walked out, passing the security guard on the way.

"We broke up. Wedding's off," then walked out the door. Almost always feels good to get in the last word.

THREE

I took my time walking back to my apartment, calling my friend Reilly on the way to tell him that I had a new case. Well, that "we" had a new case. We were long-time drinking buddies and he had helped me with some tough cases in the past. He would definitely be all over this one. He liked frequenting places like The Catwalk and spoke the language.

I got his machine and left a message. He owned a building inspection business down in the tonier part of Connecticut and had been working a lot of hours lately. Trying to support his multiple lifestyles these days wasn't cheap. He considered himself an artist and materials were expensive. And he certainly liked to imbibe. He was generous to his employees and would spring for any excuse to have a party. It used to be a concern until I realized it was useless to worry about it. He certainly didn't.

I thought about going back to the Owl again. My buzz had started to dissipate and I decided I wasn't really into it. I looked at my phone. Almost 8:00. Time for dinner.

I walked around the corner to the Shake Shack and ordered a burger and a strawberry shake, then found a corner booth where I could watch the other people who were eating there. It was mostly students at this time of night, scarfing down fast food while they stayed buried in their laptops. I shook my head and enjoyed my burger.

When I finished, I went back around the corner to go in to my apartment building when I heard a loud whistle and looked across the street and saw Reilly beckoning me over to the Owl.

The Owl was a bar and a cigar lounge. Grandfathered in when the laws changed, it was the only bar open to the public that still allowed the smoking of cigars and cigarettes. The makeup of the crowd changed from day to day. They had many regulars who were there often, a club of sorts, and Reilly and I counted ourselves as members. I walked over and stepped inside the front door.

Reilly was sitting at the front window table. The windows were open, though it was a fairly cool night. It usually meant that there was a lot of smoke inside.

He was on a tear, holding court, bouncing around on a variety of his favorite topics. I recognized a few of the other people at the table as some of the employees from his inspection business. They must have been having a meeting. Reilly liked holding them there, so he could talk business between shots. By the number of empty glasses on the table, I could tell there'd been a lot to discuss. I stood next to him and nodded hello to the other folks. His captive audience.

He put his arm around me. "Now, this guy, this guy knows a lot about a lot of stuff. T, tell me, what do you think? This guy in the White House, is he an idiot or is he sly like a fox? I say he's a moron." He was slurring his words.

I made it a point to never get into political discussions, drunk or sober, and I wasn't going to change that now.

"Here's what I think. I think you're toasted, so disregard the phone message I just left and call me mañana so we can talk. Got a case you're gonna like."

"Mañana? Mañana?" He started singing. "The sun'll come up, mañana, bet your bottom dollar, come what may!"

I put a finger to my lips and said, "Shhh. Don't sing, Annie."

He laughed but quieted down for a minute, then asked me to have a drink. I was already at my limit, although the food had helped towards sobering me up. I said no and he shrugged, then started back in on discussing the state of the world. The case would wait until tomorrow, when he was sober.

I said goodnight to all and walked back across the street and into my apartment in the Taft Hotel. No longer a hotel, it had been converted to apartments years back and now catered to students, artists and others. I was an "other." They still employed a doorman. Sort of. Ben was on duty tonight. He was in his late 70s and, more often than not, he would be asleep at his post. I nodded to him as I passed and I think he nodded back. It may have been a tic.

Once inside my apartment, I stripped down to boxers and a T-shirt, then pulled out my beat-up old laptop and sat down at the kitchen table to see what I could find out about the Catwalk Club.

There wasn't much in there I didn't already know. A few Yelp reviews, most of them over five years old. A story in the Yale newspaper that was also old. Some arrest notifications.

I would need to go there tomorrow, see it for myself, and maybe find the two people that Jessika had mentioned.

I wasn't looking forward to getting into this but who knows, maybe the sun will come up mañana...and shine a light on the whole sordid mess.

FOUR

I awoke early the next day but stayed in bed for a while, trying to remember the strange dream I'd been having. I couldn't conjure up most of it, just a blurry image of a half-naked woman spinning endlessly on a dancer pole. The image kept coming in and out. I shook it off and got out of bed.

I made a pot of strong Peet's coffee and took a shower while it brewed. I drank almost half of it while I toweled off. I was aware of feeling anxious about something and that was manifesting itself in wanting to do everything quickly. I tried slowing down.

I left the apartment and walked down to Crown Street and over to Meat and Co. to get myself a bacon and egg sandwich and a Naked Juice strawberry/banana smoothie. It was busier than it usually was and John, the owner, didn't have much time for our usual banter. I picked up my order, paid and waved at him as I left.

Eating as I walked, I continued down Crown to State Street and then turned right, until I got to Water

Street, right before the train station. Veering left, I headed up past Sports Haven, where Reilly and I usually went to watch and bet the Triple Crown each year. I took a left at East Street and kept walking until I came to the Catwalk.

The club was housed in a particularly homely building in an area of New Haven that had clearly seen better days. It felt like the city had forgotten this neighborhood entirely. Known as the Mill River section, it was primarily industrial, with low-cost housing projects that dotted the landscape. Located at the outer reaches of the Italian section of town, it had once been home to a number of great Italian restaurants and Italian grocery stores. The neighborhood took a hard hit in the 70's and the only consumer businesses there now were automotive repair shops, electrical stores and plumbing supply outlets. And the Catwalk.

The info I'd found online said they opened at 9:30 in the morning. I was hard pressed to think of anyone who would be going there that early but hoped that a manager or a bartender might be there to receive deliveries.

The front door was padlocked so I went down a narrow alley on the side of the building to the employee entrance. I knocked hard a few times until it opened. A tall, brawny guy came to the door. He had on a tight T-shirt and was clearly a body builder.

"Yeah?"

It was aggressive and I got the feeling I'd interrupted something.

"Name's Tommy Shore. Is Victor Trang in yet?"

He looked at me and I could see him thinking about

the question and how accommodating he wanted to be. He finally nodded and said, "Hang on, I'll check."

The door slammed loudly. I waited two minutes and was about to knock again when it opened and another tall guy was standing there. I wondered if there was a height requirement.

"I'm Victor. They told me you were looking for me. Whattya need?"

He looked to be in his mid-20s and was very soft spoken. It also looked like there was something going on behind the eyes. I made a mental note not to be an occupational bigot.

"I'm here about Jessika. Candy?"

He looked over his shoulder then quickly came outside, sticking a brick into the door jamb to keep it from closing completely. He took my elbow and tried to lead me back up the alley. I jerked it away out of habit and he apologized. "Sorry, man. Just want to get out of earshot of the door. Can we go out to the street?"

I nodded and we moved down the alley. He turned left when we got to the street and continued walking for 15 feet, stopping in the doorway of what had once been a hardware store. There were two dusty display windows that jutted out on each side, with room to talk in the space that led to the entrance door. He turned to me, exhaled loudly, and whispered, "Okay, now I can talk."

He was being very careful. I hadn't expected that. I plowed ahead.

"I'm a private investigator. Jessika hired me to look into her situation and told me that you know about it. She's clearly terrified. She wants me to try and find out who this mutt is and put a stop to it. Anything you can tell me would be a great help."

He looked around again. "Well, as you can imagine, we get more than our share of creeps that come in here, pretty regularly. I've tried to think if it could be one of them but I don't think so. Most of them keep to themselves, almost like they're shy. Mommy issues, right? When we spot one playing with himself or something, the bouncer gets called and they get tossed. Most go quietly. That doll thing was pretty aggressive."

I nodded. "Not to mention psychopathic. You work here full time?"

"Nah, six hours at night, three days a week. I come in to do inventory two mornings. You got me on one of those days. I go to UNH."

The University of New Haven was actually located in West Haven and was ranked third of the three schools in the area, Yale first, located downtown, and Quinnipiac second, way up in Hamden. It was the most affordable of the three colleges and geared towards the kids of blue-collar folks that made up most of the area. Given the specificity of his assessment, I was thinking he was a psych major. Maybe doing graduate work.

"How well do you know Jessika? Just from work?"

He smiled. "We've gone out for coffee a few times. Never really dated, if that's what you're asking. She's not really my type. Most times, it's together with other dancers, after our shifts. We go over to Cody's Diner. They're open pretty late."

I looked at him. He seemed like a nice enough kid but I wasn't sure he was going to be much help. I noted the need for secrecy and the whispering.

"You're pretty jumpy. Are you worried that someone's gonna see you talking to me?"

He looked around again before he spoke. I wondered if his neck was getting sore.

"Look, I'm pretty good at this job. Tony, the owner, he likes me and I like making drinks for most of the people who come into the club. It's all about how you talk to people. I'm good with them and they feel taken care of when I'm here. But there's some guys that come in that seem to be..." He hesitated and looked around again.

I prodded him on. "What?"

He was deciding how much to say. "Well, you know...connected. We get a lot of guys that come over the bridge from East Haven. Some are wannabes but a lot seem to be the real deal. I know from talking to people that the Colonna family used to be in New Haven for years. These guys look like they could be with those guys."

It wasn't something I had considered but it made sense. I'd watched enough episodes of "The Sopranos" to realize that those guys liked to frequent these places. I also thought that those "mob" days were long gone. I figured there were guys still around but that most of the older guys who once made up the sordid part of New Haven's past had died off long ago. Maybe they were making a comeback.

I gave Victor my card and asked him to call me if he thought of anything else. He took it but I wasn't sure if it would be tossed as soon as I left. He was too nervous to keep it on him or drop it where it could be found by the wrong someone in the club.

"One last question. Any chance you know if TJ's dancing tonight and when she usually gets in?"

He shrugged and shook his head that he didn't know. I would need to come back in the later hours. A tough job but someone had to do it.

FIVE

I decided to take Grand Avenue on the walk back to my place. Known as Fair Haven, this neighborhood was also bordered by the river. There were a number of historic buildings and homes that were still there but what once had been a vibrant street had also seen better days. This neighborhood had also gone through a rough period during the last part of the previous century. Businesses had closed up and the landscape had changed, some of it for the better. There were a number of terrific Hispanic restaurants and bodegas and one of the places I loved was El Coqui, a Puerto Rican take-out place. I stopped in and got an order of Alcapurria, hot fritters that were overstuffed with beef and pork and spices. My intention was to wait until I got home to eat them but I ended up finishing all three on the walk back.

This made me thirsty. It was just past noon so I stopped into the Owl. The usual bunch of saps were there, regulars who spent their lunch break having a beer and a smoke while staring at their phones. It was too early to do hard drinking so I ordered a Corona from Mike, the day bartender. Looking around, I spotted Robert Valencia, sitting in the back, reading the newspaper.

Valencia, Bobby V as he was known to almost everyone, owned a number of successful funeral parlors in New Haven, with the biggest one on Wooster Square, right in the middle of the Italian section. His places catered almost exclusively to folks from that background. The word around town was that he was once "connected" and had done funerals for a large number of prominent mob guys over the years. We knew each other from other funerals I'd attended at his places and from the Owl. I got up and went over to join him, sitting down in one of the leather chairs in front of the private cigar lockers.

He was a good-looking man, maybe in his late 60s, with a perpetual tan and a full head of hair, which he had styled three times a week. Not one was out of place. He always wore an expensive tie and a tailored shirt, typically blue with a white collar. His shoes were shined to glossy perfection. He was smart and well-spoken and I always enjoyed the conversations we had. He looked up from the paper when I sat down and smiled broadly.

"Tommy. Great to see you. You look good. How's things?"

He used the same greeting for everyone. It wasn't put on, he was sincerely interested.

"All good, Bob, all good. Staying busy. You?"

He closed the paper he had been reading. The cigar he was smoking had gone out, so he picked it up and re-lit it. Once he got it started again, he asked me if I wanted one, offering me the pick from the stash that had been lying on the table in front of him, next to the large coffee he was drinking. He always smoked expensive Davidoff Winston Churchill's that sold for over twenty dollars apiece. It was a generous offer but I declined. Briefly considered taking one for later but didn't want to appear rude. He shrugged and considered my question.

"My business, as usual, is unfortunately booming. Are you sure that I can't offer you a smoke?"

"Thanks, Bob, don't have time to partake just yet. Working a case. I actually wanted to ask you a few questions, need some info. You mind?"

He furrowed his brow. "Not sure how I can help you but I'll tell you what I can. Whattya need?"

"The case I'm trying to decide if I want to take involves the Catwalk on East Street. You know the place, right?"

He laughed. "Only by reputation and as a source of business. We've actually picked up a number of bodies there over the years. Guys get overexcited and their hearts give out. I've never been there for pleasure, though. Not really my kind of off-hours society, if you know what I mean?"

I nodded. "I do. It's a weird mix of crowd that goes there. Some are, let's say...unsavory."

He looked at me. "Ah, now I see where this conversation is going. Not sure what can I tell you, Tom, but I'll do my best. In as general a way as I can."

It had been some time since the "unsavories" had influence in this town but there were still remnants around. There were still a few private clubs near where his businesses were, and I knew they didn't look kindly on those who spoke out of turn. I respected his need to talk in code.

"I'm really looking for anything at all. My potential client is a dancer who works there. She's being stalked, getting nasty letters, threats...she seems like a nice kid but she's scared. I know that joint is frequented by guys that belong to certain organizations...might even be partners in the place. Anything you know or may have heard about in the past could help me decide if I'm going to pursue this."

He was looking down, using his torch to re-light his cigar again. When he looked up, he smiled and said, "Tom, if you haven't taken the job yet you might want to think hard about not taking it. The guys you're talking about? They're most definitely involved in that place. It's a goldmine with a ton of money flowing in and out. Practically all cash. There aren't many businesses like that anymore. Nowadays, credit is king. Jeez, I'm even taking credit cards from people who use them to pay for their funerals."

It was my turn to laugh. "Must be hard collecting on those." I refrained from making a joke about dying to pay up.

He continued, "There are still guys here in New Haven, guys that were once associated with New York. Most live over in East Haven. They're also tied into Bridgeport but a lot of that has gone away. The businesses they used to run - booze, cigarettes, gambling, and protection – it's all so regulated now that most people just go to the Indian casinos. Nobody bothers with it. Even protection is a tough nut. Owners pay such high premiums for insurance, no one wants to pay for protection. They actually hope the place gets fire-bombed so they can collect and retire."

He laughed again. "It's a different world, Tom. Makes one feel old, ya know?"

I did know. I knew it was getting tougher to make a living on the straight and narrow but now I was finding out that the old adage was true, that even crime didn't pay. You just can't count on anything anymore.

I thanked him and asked him to call me if he thought of anything else, then walked out, dropping a ten on the bar as I passed it. Mike nodded his thanks at me. I was headed back to my apartment and the possibility of a nap. The fritters were sitting in my gut and making me sleepy. I would need to go back down to the Catwalk later tonight. I would need to be well rested.

SIX

I sat and read the *Post* and the *Register* for a while, then dozed off for a couple of hours. I still hadn't heard back from Reilly. I woke up just after four and looked in the fridge to see what I could scrounge. Not a lot there. I decided on an omelet and took out some cheese and butter and eggs and light cream, then whipped it all together, with salt and pepper and a touch of tabasco. I took a couple of pieces of Italian bread that I'd bought at a little place in Hamden called The Venice. They made it fresh every day and it was delicious, toasted or untoasted. I decided to toast it and when it was done, I lathered it up with French butter and sat down to eat. I tried to pace myself by reading the paper between bites but I finished in record time, it was that good.

Around six, I left the apartment and went back across the street to the Owl, this time for a real drink. Priming the pump, so to speak. For some reason, I was feeling unusually anxious about going to the strip club and wasn't sure why. I'd been to them before, even went to a famous one in New York once, the inevitable part of a bachelor party. The place was one of those fancy deals, String Fellows or some such pretentious name and was supposedly where Bruce Willis had tended bar some twenty years before becoming a star. I remembered that the drinks were expensive, the bottles even more so, and that all the girls looked bored to tears.

At the Owl, I sat at the front window table, ordered a Jameson and lit up a Hemingway Short Story. A bunch of customers filed in, none regulars I could recognize. Nobody waved to me or stopped to say hello and shake hands. It used to be a collegial place but it was changing.

After an hour and a half or so, I got the check, paid, and headed down to the Catwalk. It was a solid 20-minute walk and I was sweating by the time I got there. I stopped in the little alcove where I had talked to Victor, trying to cool down. I needed to ask questions and it wouldn't be easy if I looked like just another moist creep.

After five minutes or so, I ran my fingers through my hair to straighten it up, then went to the entrance door. The cover charge was minimal, ten bucks. It was dark inside once I entered and it took a few minutes for my eyes to adjust.

It was still early, just past 8:00. A few guys were sitting at the tables near the runway and Motley Crüe was blasting from the speakers that hung in each corner of the place, with the volume turned to 11. Seemed appropriate. A few of the vampires at the bar turned to check out the fresh blood, then turned quickly back to the girls.

A black girl with platinum white hair was sitting on the edge of the stage, naked except for a frilly panty type thing that was stuffed with bills. She was finishing her routine and I heard the announcer asking for "a big hand for Fantasia." There was a smattering of applause. I found a seat at the bar.

There were two bartenders working. One was Jessika's friend Victor, who I could see down at the far end of the bar. He glanced at me and tried not be noticed doing it. He still seemed nervous.

The bartender on my end was an extremely buxom young lady, maybe 22, with short brown hair, Kristen Stewart meets Pam Anderson. Wearing high heels, shiny silk boxing shorts and a vest. Nothing more. I could see she was very tan. She had a name tag on that said Jennifer.

I smiled at her and said, "Jennifer. Some of my favorite actresses are named Jennifer."

Small talk was not always my forte but she laughed anyway.

"Yeah? Like who?"

"Hmm...Connelly. Kidman. Lopez."

She frowned. "Lopez?"

"Yeah, she did that cop show on TV. She was pretty good."

She laughed and nodded. "Okay, I believe you. What can I get you to drink?"

I looked at the beer list on the bar and ordered a Red Stripe. She reached down into the cooler in front of where I was sitting and there was nothing left to the imagination. I was guessing she made a good living from tips. She pulled an opener from her vest pocket, popped off the cap, put it in front of me and asked me if I wanted to start a tab. I told her I would pay as I went.

"Okay, great. That'll be $15." I narrowed my eyes at her and she just shrugged. I gave her a twenty and told her to keep the change. I would drink slowly.

I looked around the place. It was definitely early in the evening by strip club standards and there were only a few guys scattered around at the tables. Except for one with five guys sitting in a room that was slightly separated from the rest of the club. Each guy was dressed in a suit but no one was wearing a tie. They weren't loud exactly but there was a boisterous aspect to the group. Cock of the walk confidence. A couple of the girls from the club were sitting with them and they had at least two large ice buckets on the side, with multiple bottles sticking out of them.

I motioned for Jennifer and she came over. I pointed at the alcove and asked her, "What's the deal over there? New Haven elite?" She looked to where I was pointing and smiled.

"Those guys? Those are regulars. Friends of the owners. They're here a couple times a week. Drop serious cash. Those bottles alone go for about $300 each."

I gave a short whistle and said, "Must be hedge fund guys or something like that?"

She shrugged again. "Maybe...but I don't think so. I used to have that table before I got behind the bar. Most of those guys couldn't tell a hedge fund from a hedgehog."

I laughed. "Trust fund babies?"

She stage-whispered "cold" and then pushed the

side of her nose a little and said, "Bada-bing guys... know what I mean?"

I nodded that I did but furrowed my eyebrows. "Really?"

She shrugged again. It was her go-to move. "So I hear. Like I said, they're friends with the owners so we don't ask many questions. I'm pretty sure they're connected. Lots of their buddies come here on a regular basis. Most times they don't even pay. But they tip great."

She walked away to wait on another customer.

I let it sink in. It was surprising, in that it was the third time today it was mentioned. All my notions that these guys no longer had a hard reign over the city came into question and my assumption that it was long ago and far away no longer seemed to play.

I finished my beer and pushed the empty to the edge of the bar. Jennifer came over again and asked if I wanted another.

"I'll need to get a second mortgage first if I want to drink here. You take care."

I gave her a little salute and she smiled.

I turned to leave then turned back. "Hey, do you know when TJ works?" She looked at me for a few seconds, considering the question.

"Do you know her?"

"I know a friend of hers. Just wanted to introduce myself."

She hesitated again, then leaned closer. I leaned in as well. "Not supposed to give out personal info but I think she's on tomorrow night. Come by. I'll be here." She winked and I saluted her again.

"Might just do that. Nice to meet you, Jennifer."

I left out the side door. I'd called an Uber from the bar and the guy was already waiting for me. I got in and gave him my address and we took off. I didn't see the car that came out from a driveway on the side of the club or notice that it followed us to my apartment.

SEVEN

I tried to sleep when I got home but my mind was racing with the possibility that there could be some kind of mob aspect to this. I had no real reason to suspect that but the thought intrigued me.

I had been thinking it was most likely some creep who had a crush on a stripper because she gave him a lap dance once. Forgetting that he paid for it, he falls in lust, only to eventually realize that it was just a business transaction and not an actual "love connection." Thwarted romantic gestures can play hard on a psyche, especially a damaged one, and this was probably the guy's angry attempt at leveling the playing field.

Now I was thinking there could be more to it.

I went online and started researching the history of the mob in New Haven. There was a lot more there than there had been on the Catwalk.

It was heady stuff. I read about a thriving underworld society that dominated the city for many years in the 1940's and 50s. I read about Billy Grasso and Midge Renault, nasty guys who ran nasty crews. It was a side of the city I knew very little about. New Haven and Bridgeport were essentially extensions of New York as far as the mob was concerned. Great fortunes had been amassed on the backs of its citizenry, through blackmail, violence, gambling, theft, extortion and fear.

I read about corrupt politicians. There was even a moment in time when the state had been dubbed "Corrupticut," so named because the mayors in towns like Bridgeport, Waterbury and Danbury had all been caught with their hands in one till or another... all the way up to the governor, who had been found guilty of taking bribes and ended up doing real time.

I read about union bosses, where the corruption ranged in scope from construction to manufacturing to the police... town after town, right up to the capital.

I read about the jai alai frontons that were built in Hartford, Milford and Bridgeport, with direct connections to Whitey Bolger and the Boston mob. No state other than Florida welcomed the sport like this one did and in a short time those guys made millions off them. Rumors of fixed games, coupled with the Indian casinos coming into the state, dealt the game a major blow and all three frontons closed after a few years.

The New Haven boys had been heavily involved there and the loss of that revenue stream took its toll. At the same time, the state was starting to shake off its puritanical background and a large number of adult bookstores and movie houses had started popping up. And, of course, strip clubs.

The Catwalk was such a place. I couldn't find the transaction papers but I found an article in an old *New Haven Register* that mentioned the purchase by an LLC named Cinzano Enterprises. Subtle.

My reverie was interrupted by a loud rapping on the door. It startled me. I looked through the peephole and saw that it was Reilly. I opened the door and the stench of booze wafted in long before he entered.

"Jesus, you smell like a still. You drink it or pour it over your head as cologne?"

He was reeling in place, slurred "I need a couch," found mine and fell down hard on it. He was asleep and snoring in seconds.

I shut everything down and found an extra blanket in the closet. He stirred when I threw it over him, turned quickly, mumbled "Oy" one last time, then fell back to sleep.

The case would have to wait until the morning. Again

EIGHT

I awoke early the next day, called Jessika and told her I would take the job. We agreed to meet later that afternoon for coffee at Willoughby's, a small indie coffee shop near State Street. Her shift didn't start until 7 that evening so we would have plenty of time to talk.

I went over to the couch and kicked at one of Reilly's boots. He stirred and turned his back to me. I caught another whiff of whiskey, still strong on him. He grunted.

"C'mon man, get up and take a shower. Are you taking a sick day? If you are, you can't stay here. There are clean towels in the closet next to the bathroom. I'm going out for coffee and some bagels." He grunted again.

He couldn't eat gluten but would occasionally eat a yogurt or some fruit for breakfast. I took a shot. "You want me to get you anything?"

"Coffee. Espresso. A double." Mumbled from beneath the blanket.

I laughed, said "Yes, sir" and walked out, making sure to let the door slam. I needed him up and out.

I walked outside and breathed in deeply, trying to shake the fumes and stuffiness of the apartment. I stretched a little but when I turned to look down College Street, I noticed a car parked there that looked out of place. Most of the traffic on that street at that time of the morning was delivery trucks, bringing food and booze replenishments to the restaurants and clubs. This looked like a new Cadillac, with the engine running. I took out my notebook and jotted down the license plate. I started to walk towards it but when I got within twenty feet, the driver took off. He barely missed hitting one of the trucks as he sped down College, then turned up Crown, tires screeching. I looked at the numbers on the pad and called my friend Jimmy.

James Wilmot was a New Haven cop. I'd met him through Reilly's sister, Kathy, at one of Reilly's infamous "blackout" parties. Every few months, Reilly would turn off the power in his apartment, light a few hundred candles, scatter a few dozen glow sticks around, and invite a bunch of girls who fancied themselves as models to come over and pose in unusual makeup, recreating bizarre scenarios. Much of the Owl crowd came, too. It was always a hoot.

The party that Kathy brought Jim to was the night when things almost got out of hand. There was a lot of drinking, a fair number of edible brownies, and some crazy behavior. The cops inevitably came, and even though he was off duty, Jimmy stepped up and handled it. It was impressive and afterwards, I told him as much. We ended up spending much of the rest of the party talking about boxing, books, music and movies. We had similar tastes in all of those things and, apart from the occasional angry glance from Kathy, it was practically a date. We stayed in touch afterwards and he even threw some job leads my way, a few divorce cases and the like. He also said that if I needed anything, to give him a call. I hadn't taken him up on it until now.

The phone rang four or five times. I was about to hang up when I heard someone fumble with the phone and then answer it. A child's voice said "Hello?"

It surprised me. I knew he was divorced but I thought his kids were older. I asked for Jimmy.

A few seconds later, he got on the phone. "Yeah, who's this?"

"Jimmy. It's Tommy Shore."

"Hey...Tommy! How ya doin', man? Been a while. What's going on?"

"Living the dream, brother, livin' the dream. Hey, I need a favor. Can you run a license for me?"

He laughed. "So much for small talk and foreplay. Sure, text it to me and give me an hour or so. I'm just leaving my sister's place to go to work."

"Thanks. I owe you a dinner. Definitely been too long."

"Agreed. Hey, you seen Kathy? Been a while since I spoke with her."

I hesitated. I made it a rule not to get involved in matters of the heart unless they were my own.

"I haven't seen much of her. I think she's been traveling. Reilly hasn't said anything but it's been a while for me, too. Maybe we should get something on the calendar?"

Already saying more than I wanted. He jumped at it.

"Definitely! Let's do that. Soon. In the meantime, I'll call ya as soon as I have the info on the plate."

I said thanks and hung up. I texted the plate number, then walked down to the bodega on Crown and grabbed two bagels with extra cream cheese and two large espressos.

Sleuthing and dodging matchmaking opportunities always made me hungry.

NINE

Reilly was up when I got back, dressed and sitting at the kitchen table, holding his head in his hands. I looked at him and shook my head.

"It's about time. Man, you look like crap. There's Extra Strength Tylenol in the bathroom, if you want." I handed him his coffee.

His eyes were barely open. He twisted the lid off and took a long swig, gulping down almost half of it, groaning, "Damn, that's hot...but great. Thanks."

I watched him. "Yeah, no worries. Hey, look, I'm the last guy to talk but you gotta get a handle on the drinking. You're getting wasted every day. You okay?"

He didn't answer for a few minutes. When he finally looked up, I could see how tired he was.

"I'm just exhausted. I feel sick all the time and no one can tell me what's wrong. I've been to six fuckin' doctors and not one knows what this shit is." He sounded exasperated. "I can't take any time off 'cause I'm short-handed on the jobs as it is and it's all I can do to find the energy to get through the day. Drinking dampens the misery."

I took a deep breath. I could see he was in a dark place. It was usually better to wait it out when he was in this kind of mood, but I knew telling him about the case might snap him out of his funk.

"Hey, let me tell you about my new client. You'll feel better."

I went through every detail, starting with Jessika at the bar, the two visits to the club, how nervous Victor was and why, and ended up with my seeing the car that took off and sped down the street when I spotted it. As expected, he was immediately intrigued and came alive, excited.

"Oi! That's fuckin' tremendous! Strippers! Well, we definitely need to go down there, right now, stake the place out. That creep will eventually show himself and we'll be all over him like white on rice!"

I didn't want him getting too excited this early and put up both my hands to slow him down a bit.

"Whoa, Hoss. Slow your roll. I'm not sure this is actually like it seems on the surface. Like I mentioned, there seems to be a dark side to this that ratchets up the danger element a notch or two."

He looked at me and sneered. "Huh. The bent noses making you nervous?"

Excitement turning to bile. It was as much a challenge as it was a taunt. I took my time answering.

"They are. You'd have to be an idiot not to at least consider it. At first, I thought those guys were over, not around New Haven anymore at the very least, but if that's not the case, I think it would be smart to proceed with caution. You don't agree?"

He made a noise that was neither a yes or no and just kept looking at me.

"You don't?"

The message icon on my phone started vibrating. Saved by the bell. I looked down and saw it was a text from Jim Wilmot.

"I gotta take this. It's the info I've been waiting for to see who that car is registered to."

I opened the text. The car was registered to one Anthony Delmonico. I texted back my thanks and asked if he knew him or anything about him. A few minutes later I got back, "Nothing good. Watch yourself." It sent a shiver down my spine.

I opened up my laptop and googled the name. My worries were confirmed. Delmonico used to be a small-time hood with big aspirations but now had some serious connections. He had turned "businessman" a few years back. There had been a few articles in the *Register* on some of the projects in Bridgeport that he had been involved with where there had been union problems. There were also intimations about his involvement with the Bridgeport mayor. The guy that ended up going to prison for corruption, served his time, then got out and was re-elected. The Delmonico name touched on many edges.

Things were starting to get intense and interesting. In the Chinese curse sort of way. I needed to get more information quickly but didn't feel like I could ask Wilmot to provide it. It was still a fairly new friendship and I wasn't ready to trust it that much yet. I opted to call Mickey Dunn instead.

While Mickey wasn't exactly what one would call a 'friend," I trusted him more than most. We'd met after we were both sentenced to community service for letting our tempers get the best of us. The judge told us we needed to go to a neighborhood school and talk with kids who were in danger of taking the wrong paths. We both found a symbiosis in the way we saw the world: that most people were schmucks and that there was a handful that weren't. We each decided that the other one wasn't one and we ended up going out for coffee after it ended.

I realized straight off that Mickey was a force to be reckoned with. Most people looked at him and saw a quiet, threatening power and were sensibly afraid. He could look at you in a way that would make you fear that he was going to hurt you. I never really felt that and over the years he had been one of my key go-to sources when I needed info. A way to reach into the underbelly of the city. Not really friends but respectful of each other.

He answered on the first ring. "Tommy boy. Been a while. Was thinking about you the other day. How goes the battle?"

That was him. Put it out there but never explain it.

"It goes, Mick, it goes. Gotta jumpstart it occasionally but it goes. I'm good, though. Working a case with lots of questions coming up around it. Was hoping you might be able to help answer some of them for me."

No hesitation. "Of course, kid. When have I ever refused you? Whattya need?"

I took a deep breath.

"Do you know anything about Anthony Delmonico?"

There was a pause, then, "Not on the phone. Let's meet. Usual place?"

I knew he meant the Owl.

"That'll work. What time?"

"I can be there in three hours. Find a place in the back, away from the hordes, Yeah?"

I agreed and hung up. Reilly was staring at me.

I stared back then shrugged. "What?"

"You're getting him involved?" Said with real anger. I knew Reilly wasn't a fan.

I scowled. "Like we have a choice? If anyone knows about these guys, it's him, no? Besides, I'm looking to err on the side of caution. Not sure why, but the stakes feel high on this one. Okay?"

He sneered again, got up, coughed hard a few times, then walked out of the apartment, slamming the door. I was pretty sure I didn't have his approval.

I sat down and ate my breakfast. There was a little time so I folded the blanket Reilly had been using, took that and his pillow and tossed them both into the hall closet. I straightened the apartment up a bit and washed the dishes. After a while, I called Jessika again, got her voice mail, and left a message that I couldn't meet her at the coffee shop but that she should call me so we could reschedule. I washed my face and hands at the kitchen sink, grabbed my pea coat, locked up, and walked across the street to the Owl.

TEN

The Owl was busy with the usual lunch crowd. I looked for the seats Mickey wanted but there was nothing available. I waited until a couple having a coffee left from one of the high tops upfront, directly across from the bar. Allie was waitressing and came over as soon as I sat down.

"What'll it be, handsome?"

She was a good-looking kid, maybe 25 or 26, with a powerful looking body and what my uncle used to call "a great rack." She'd been at some of Reilly's parties and even modeled a few times for his themed photo shoots. Often accompanied by her latest beau. And while she didn't have the best taste in men, she loved to flirt. I liked her a lot.

"Just a Corona. Lemon instead of lime? Thanks, doll. "

I checked my phone to see if Jessika had called me back. Nothing. Allie came back with the beer, placed it down in front of me and winked. It made me laugh.

A few minutes late Mickey walked in.

He was short but compact, like a bulldog. And although he was on the other side of 60, he was very fit and clearly well-muscled beneath his bespoke suit. People cleared a path for him as he made his way towards my table.

"Not really in the back now, is it?"

I laughed. "Busy here. People back there seemed pretty dug in."

He glanced towards the back. "Be right back."

I watched him walk back to the two farthest seats, where a young couple was sitting. On his way, he caught the attention of Allie and whispered in her ear. When he reached the couple, he leaned in and spoke to them and they immediately got up and walked towards me as Mickey sat down in one of the vacated chairs. When they got to the table, I got up, grabbed my beer, and heard the guy say, "Thanks." I walked back to Mickey and asked him, "What happened there?"

He smirked a little. "I made them a deal that you would buy their lunch if they swapped with us, so we could talk in private. They seemed open to it."

I laughed. Mickey was a whiz at getting what he wanted, through intimidation or OPP – other people's pockets. I sat down and started telling him what was going on.

He listened intently and said nothing. There was no perceptible response when I mentioned Delmonico's name but I felt as though the intensity of his stare had grown stronger. Might have been my imagination. When I was done, he didn't say anything for a few minutes. Allie had brought the two espressos Mickey had ordered and he was slowly sipping at one. I picked up my beer and took a sizeable swig, trying to catch up. He finally put the cup down and looked at me.

"Tom, Delmonico is bad news. He's basically a punk who's watched 'The Godfather' one too many times and thinks he's Sonny Corleone. Everyone always forgets what happened to Sonny. Delmonico's father was a bigshot once with a local crew, a capo. They ran the rackets here, took betting slips and provided protection in New Haven for a lot of years. When Anthony was born, his family treated him like royalty, bringing him around and introducing him, like he was the heir to the throne. It went to his head but it never happened the way they thought it would. There were territory disputes and major fights between Bridgeport and New Haven."

I took it all in. "What happened to the old man?"

Mickey took a sip. "No one's seen him in over 20 years. Here one day, gone the next. And nobody ever said anything more about it. Just business."

It surprised me. This was the stuff from the movies, here in my own backyard. Everything I'd read online said New Haven was no longer a mob town but evidently, it had just gone underground. I told Mickey what I'd read and asked him about the history.

"New Haven really only had a few really bad guys that ran things. Like Bridgeport, we had the harbor and we had the docks. There was a ton of merchandise flowing through Long Wharf and the surrounding areas. It's also the halfway point between NYC and Boston. It was ripe for the picking."

I nodded. I knew about Bridgeport, 30 miles closer to New York, but always thought that New Haven was far enough away that it wasn't feasible. Hearing Mickey tell it differently made a lot of sense.

He took a final sip of his espresso. "Listen, kiddo, whatever you do here, be careful. The word is Anthony's not right in the head. After the father disappeared, he got pushed way down in the organization and eventually became a punch line to a lot of jokes the other guys made, especially those looking to make a name for themselves. It ruined him, made him even crazier than he already was. He was always a hothead but now he had something to prove. Made some wrong moves that the top bosses didn't like and got shut down by them as a result. He's been trying to put together his own thing for years now."

He stood up to leave. "By the way, Delmonico owns that club you're looking into, the Catwalk. Nothing on the books, just one day it was owned by some legit guys and the next day it was his."

I took it all in. "Mick, thank you. As always, good info and advice. I will definitely watch my back."

He smiled, tight and a little scary. "I think he still hangs out at his little private club on Wooster. You know, a few guys that sit around and bullshit, playing cards and drinking espresso. One big, fat cliché."

He took out a twenty and tried to hand it to me but I waved him off. "I got this."

He nodded thanks and said, "One more thing, Tommy. The word on the street about this mutt is that he has a thing for strippers. There's talk that he has the final say on who gets hired to work at the place but that the girls all have to audition for him before they can work. And that he's not used to hearing no for an answer. Understand?"

I nodded that I did and stood up. We shook hands and he left. I watched as the crowd moved aside as he went out the door. I signaled Allie and she came right over. I ordered a double Jameson, straight up. I felt like I was going to need it.

ELEVEN

When I got back to my apartment, the light on the phone was blinking. There were four messages, all from Jessika. Each one sounded more upset than the last.

I called her back and she picked up the phone on the first ring. All I heard was crying, then wheezing as she tried to catch her breath. I tried to calm her down.

"Jessika, breathe, deep and easy. Slow down, so I can help you. What happened?"

She tried to talk but she was too worked up and I couldn't understand her.

"Where are you? Do you want me to come there?"

I could barely make out the soft "Yes" of her response.

"Okay, you have my cell, text me the address and I'll be right there. Fifteen minutes, tops."

Hoping that she lived reasonably close.

I hung up and threw my coat back on, then left the apartment. The address came through on the walk out the front door and luck had it that a cab was parked on the corner of Chapel. She lived up in the Westville neighborhood, a slightly upscale area that had been going through gentrification for the last 20 years. I told the cabbie there was extra cash in it for him if he could get me there in a hurry. It was met with a sigh and an unconvincing, "Sure" but he actually hustled and we pulled up to her building in under fifteen minutes. I threw a $20 bill at him and said, "Keep it." I exited to another sigh.

Jessika's building was fairly modern, built in the last few years. I seemed to remember an appliance store that had been on this corner or maybe a 7-11. Regardless, whatever had been here before had been razed and a building that held eight small apartments had been put up in its stead. From the front, it didn't look like it would take a whole lot of huffing or puffing to bring it down.

I rang the bell for #7, as instructed on the text. The door buzzed open and I took the stairs on the right two at a time to the second floor. Her apartment was down the hall.

When I knocked on the door, Victor answered immediately. I must have looked slightly surprised because he quickly told me that he had just gotten there, that she had reached out to him when she couldn't get hold of me the first few times she called.

"It's bad, man. Guy's been escalating things up. She got another box at the club. This one had a dead cat in it. Lots of blood. Must have been dead a while. Smelled horrendous. It was waiting for her in the dressing room after her set. She's freaked out."

I could tell from the clipped way he was telling me this that he was a little "freaked out" as well. Understandable. Stalking and violent threats aren't in most people's wheelhouse. At least, not the ones that aren't sociopaths.

I brushed past him, asking "Where is she?" He pointed at a door I assumed was her bedroom. I knocked softly and said, "Jessika? It's Tommy. I'm coming in."

She was sitting on the bed, wearing flannel pajamas and holding a teddy bear. She looked like a little kid. A very frightened little kid. She started crying again when she saw me.

I sat down on the bed and waited for her to get control of herself. She reached out and took my hand and I looked at her face closely. This thing was taking a toll on her. Her skin looked sallow and there were dark circles under her eyes. Her nose was running and she was heaving, as her heart raced. My sense was that she wasn't going to be easily consoled but I'd give it a try. I summoned up a smile and spoke to her in a soft voice.

"Hey. Jess. I'm here now. You're safe. I can stick around for as long as you need me. And Victor's here, too."

Her eyes widened and she started apologizing for calling him. I put my hand up and shook my head.

"It's fine. You do whatever you need to do in order to not feel afraid, it's all okay. He seems like a good friend."

She nodded, absentmindedly. I wanted to get her focused so I could get some details.

"Can you talk? Do you need water?"

She shook her head to the water, then started nodding. "I can talk." She hadn't let go of my hand.

"Great. Tell me what happened."

She took a deep breath.

"After I got your message that we weren't meeting, I went in to work early, just to sit and try to get my head straight. I've been trying to meditate lately, using some tips that I found on YouTube. It seemed to help. There was nothing in the dressing room when I got there besides the usual trash. You know, old makeup, clothes that had been tossed around, magazines. Nothing out of the ordinary. I would have noticed the box. At the very least, I would have smelled it, right? It was horrible."

She sniffed loudly.

"Anyway, I got called up for my first set and left the dressing room. I was only on stage for fifteen, twenty minutes, tops, but when I came back, the box was sitting on the dressing table. I could smell it before I saw it. I didn't notice the blood running down the back of it. When I opened it, I saw it was a dead animal. I screamed and both bouncers came running. It was horrible."

Her nose was still running. I reached over and grabbed a tissue from the box on a table near the bed. She finally let go of my hand, took the Kleenex, blew her nose into it, then gently dabbed at her eyes with it.

I prodded her to go on. "Then what happened?"

She looked up and I could see she was confused. "What do you mean? Brian, one of the bouncers, said it was a dead cat. I was freaked out. They called me an Uber and I came straight home. When I couldn't reach you, I called Victor." She pointed her chin at the doorway. I turned to see Victor leaning in the doorway. I hadn't realized he was standing there. He straightened up when she mentioned his name.

"Do you still want me to stay?"

I wasn't sure whether he was asking her or me. She

looked at me and shrugged. I stood up and said I'd be right back, then guided Victor out to the living room.

"Anything to add here? Were you working?"

He shook his head. "No, night off. Had a date but she bailed on me, last minute. I was eating cold pizza and watching a movie when Jessika called."

I nodded. I was familiar with the single life.

I wanted to know how the owners reacted. "Look, I'm pretty sure they wouldn't call the cops but what do you think Tony would do about this? One time's a nuisance but this graduates it up to being a real problem. Do you know if he called anyone about it?"

Victor shook his head and shrugged. "I know they wouldn't be happy. It meant someone got backstage and got into the dressing room. That's a major security breach."

I scowled at him. "Not to mention terrorizing one of their employees."

He corrected himself immediately. "Oh yeah, of course...but you know these guys. They think the people who work for them are disposable, especially the girls. There's always another body available to take her place. No, they'll be pissed about somebody going behind the curtain."

Unless it was one of their own and they already knew who was doing it. I changed the subject. "When I was there a few days ago, when you saw me, I noticed there was a hidden camera in the middle of the bar. I imagine it's there for watching the registers but they can capture a fair amount of the room sometimes. Do you think Tony would let me have access to it or would he want to protect his clientele?

I tried not to spit that last word out, not wanting to

let my disdain for the people who frequented those places color my attitude towards the employees.

Victor frowned and swallowed hard. "What camera?"

I laughed. You would need to know what you were looking for to see it. It made sense they didn't let the bartenders know it was there. "Over the bar. Take my word, there's a camera there. Do you think they'd have a problem with me seeing the footage?"

He was still processing that there was a camera watching him when he worked. I could see him going over it in his head, trying to remember if there might be anything that he did that might bite him on the ass. I asked again, a bit harsher. "Victor, focus. I'm thinking about trying to talk to the owners, convince them to let me look at the footage. What do you think are my chances?"

He looked up. "Huh. Yeah, yeah, you should talk to Tony. Tony Aprillo. Fat Tony. He's the easier one to talk to of the two bosses. You might be able to reason with him. I can call him and tell him you're coming down."

I smiled. "Great. Can you hang here for a while?" I took out some cash and dropped 40 dollars on the kitchenette counter. "Maybe get some food for the two of you? I'll be back in a few hours but don't leave the apartment. Have the food delivered."

I could tell that he didn't really want to stay. That last tidbit about the camera made him nervous but I also knew that he didn't want to get on my bad side. I can have that effect sometimes. I handed him my phone. "Put your cell phone number in there, in case I need to reach you." He did as I asked.

I went back into the bedroom to talk to Jessika. She was rocking back and forth, in the same spot on the bed as when I left her.

"Listen, kiddo, I'm going down to the club to check some things out and see if I can get some ideas about who's doing this to you. Victor will stay with you until I get back. I left him money for food. He's going to get some takeout delivered. You should eat something. I'll be back in a couple of hours."

Her eyes got wide and I could see that she wanted me to stay but understood that I couldn't find the bad guy if I stayed there. She looked down and nodded. "Please hurry?"

I said I would and left, calling a Lyft car on my way down the stairs.

TWELVE

I had the driver stop at my apartment first so I could get a gym bag and a change of clothes. I also grabbed my sap. I'd bought it years before while on a trip to Dublin and smuggled it back home. It was perfectly weighted and had come in quite handy over the years. I hoped I wouldn't need it.

The driver was waiting where I left him and took me down to the Catwalk. I got out of the car and walked in the first door, paid the cover charge, then walked through a second door. There was a bouncer standing at both entrances. I told the second bouncer my name and asked if Tony was around and that Victor had called about me. He looked me up and down a few times then told me I would need to leave my bag with the coat check girl, pointing down a hall to a half door with a lovely but slightly overweight young lady leaning on it from the inside, reading a book. I chuckled and walked over to her.

"Hi. I understand you have to check this?"

She looked up without expression, took the bag

from me, and then put it on a wire rack above the hanging coats. I glanced down at the book she had been reading. *Of Mice and Men*. When she handed me my ticket, I said, "Trouble with mice is you always kill 'em." She looked at me as if I had two heads. It was all I could do to refrain from spoiling it and telling her that George kills Lennie in the end.

I went back to Bouncer #2, who took me into the club, past the bar and through a door that lead to a long hallway. We walked by a room that had to be the dressing room where the package had been left. The door was open slightly and a few of the girls were in there, waiting for their next big shot at show business.

At the end of the hallway was a door marked OFFICE. Bouncer #2 knocked on it, three short raps and I heard a gruff voice call out "Yeah?" #2 announced me and I could hear a rustling noise and some brisk movement, along with a grumbled, "Hang on." The door opened and a young lady came out, looking at the ground and shuffled past us. I watched her go into the dressing room. I was shown in and introduced to Tony, who was sitting behind his desk, trying to hide the state of arousal he was in and failing miserably. We had interrupted something.

"Just in the middle of a conversation with one of my dancers. What can I do for you, Mr. Shore?" Surprisingly cordial, considering.

I could see where the nickname came from. He wasn't tall but he probably went 300 pounds, with an enormous gut that flopped over his pants and hid his belt.

"Tommy. I'm actually working for one of your dancers, Jessika. I'm sure you're familiar with what's happened to her twice now, and I was told you might be the guy I should talk to in order to get some help looking into it."

"Told by whom?" Not aggressive, just getting the facts.

"Victor. He's a friend of Jessika's and she called him to be with her after this last incident. She couldn't reach me so she called him. He seems like a straight shooter."

Tony scoffed. "Yeah, well, not sure how straight he is but that figures. They've always been too chummy when they worked together. Never been an issue, though. I'm pretty sure she doesn't feel threatened by him, if you know what I mean?"

I could see that Tony wasn't a fan of Victor's. I nodded to move the conversation along. It felt like subtlety would be lost on this guy so I decided to come right out and ask him for what I needed.

"I was here a few days ago, sat at the bar, and noticed you have a camera hidden there. I'm assuming it's there to keep the staff honest but I was wondering if you might let me take a look at the footage from the last 24 hours or so? Not sure what I'll see but you never know, something might stick out that sets off some alarms. I'm sure you must be worried that whoever left this second package for Jessika got backstage. Might be worthwhile for you as well."

I didn't mention that Victor thought they'd be more concerned about the security breach than about Jess.

"Huh. That's impressive, Tommy, you spotting that camera. I thought I did a good job of hiding it. Yeah, we've had some issues with money missing so the owners pretty much said I needed to find out what was going on and put a stop to it or I'd be gone. I haven't caught anyone dipping into the kitty and the issues have stopped. I didn't tell anyone about the camera but you know how places like this operate, word gets around pretty quickly. But you spotting it, that's pretty good."

I thanked him for the compliment. "Well, you know how it is, Tony, you do a thing long enough, you get good at it. 10,000 hours and all that. Right?"

He nodded like he understood me but I could have been speaking Latin.

I pushed a little. "Besides, I thought you owned the joint?"

He rolled his eyes. "I wish. On paper maybe. There's another party involved that's got the lion's share of it."

I feigned ignorance but let it drop. "So, whattya say, can we take a look?"

He seemed like the kind of guy who liked to do favors for people so he could keep it in his back pocket for when he'd need it back. Tenfold.

"Not a problem. I got the footage here." He turned and grabbed a small stack of VHS tapes from a shelf behind him. I hadn't seen those in a while and may have smirked, which he noticed.

"Yeah, I know, it's old school, using a VCR, but I'm not a fan of those DVD things."

Buying the hardware must have come out of his pocket.

I smiled and tried collegial. "Hey, whatever works, right?"

He nodded. "Exactly. Let's see what we got." He walked over to a small TV with a VCR below it that was in the corner of the office. He made an effort to squat down to insert the tape that had been on the top of the pile into the slot and hit the ON button for the television. The TV popped on and there was snow for a minute, with a time stamp in the corner. Finally, a picture of the bar came into view. Tony grabbed the remote and fast-forwarded it to 8:00 last night then handed me the remote.

"Knock yourself out," then went back to his desk.

I watched for a few minutes, fast-forwarding ahead to see if anything struck me, but realized it was useless trying to do this here. I needed to spend time going through it with someone who might know some of the faces.

"Any way that I can borrow this?" Taking a shot.

Tony looked at me for a few seconds, then shrugged. "Sure. Take it. I went through it already. Most of the action happens around 10:30, anyway."

I frowned. It was a strange thing to say. He had evidently watched it already and checked for anything incriminating. I let it slide.

"Thanks, I'll get it back to you as soon as I can."

He shook his head. "Nah, no need. Got a great deal on 'em at the Dollar store. 20 for ten bucks. Bought a hundred."

I laughed. "Quite the bargain. Well, thanks again. I'll let myself out."

He waved me out and was already on the intercom, calling the dressing room. Probably to continue his "conversation" with the dancer. I nodded at the young lady as we passed in the hall, refraining from wishing her a good night.

I felt it was already too late for that.

THIRTEEN

I walked back through the bar and glanced around. No one jumped up and claimed responsibility for sending the packages so I went out to the vestibule, got my bag back from the coat check girl, threw a buck in the little basket, then called for another Uber. I waited just inside the first entrance, under the watchful eye of both bouncers. Guess they only let psychopathic stalkers in without surveillance.

When my ride arrived, the car was being driven by a very large, very round black woman, who was blasting Nat King Cole from the CD player. I had her drive me back to Jessika's place and got out as "It's Only a Paper Moon" started up. I almost asked her to go around the block again.

Victor buzzed me in and opened the door when I knocked. I walked in and threw my bag on the couch. He started whining right away.

"I've been checking on her regularly. She's asleep now. There was a lot of crying. It drove me crazy so I gave her a couple of Tylenol PMs and a glass of wine. It knocked her right out."

I snorted at that. "Yeah, better living through chemistry. Anything else happen? Phone ring?"

He shook his head. "No, that was it. I was watching a movie when you rang the doorbell."

I walked into the kitchen and looked around. A pizza box lay on the counter. "Pizza guy come up to the apartment?"

He shook his head again. "No, I went down. Thought it would be better, in case someone was watching him and tried to brace the guy for the apartment number when he left."

I chuckled at the word "brace." Everybody wants to be on "Law and Order."

"Okay. You did a good job. You're a good friend. I'll take it from here. You can leave."

I saw his head jerk back slightly and realized I had been abrupt.

"Hey, I'm sorry. I'm meant that I'm good here with her for the time being. You don't have to hang out. You must have other stuff to do, right? I may need you later on, if you're around. When's your next shift?"

He nodded but still seemed disappointed.

"I'm working tomorrow night, 6 to close. Open all day."

He sounded sulky. I had second thoughts about his feelings for Jessika.

"Look, I'll call you if I need you. I promise. You did a good job."

I clapped him on the shoulder and pushed him towards the door. I had things to do and didn't need to babysit him as well. He finally got the hint and left.

I called Reilly. He answered on third ring, saying. "Columbo! How goes the crime fighting biz?"

I had no time for sarcastic chitchat.

"It goes. Hey, do you still have a VCR that works? I want to bring Jess there. I'm here at her apartment but it's not safe and neither is mine. I need to hide her out somewhere. Can I bring her to your place in an hour?"

To his credit, he didn't ask any questions, said that he did have a VCR that works and that I could bring her there if I thought it was absolutely necessary. It was clear he wasn't happy with the scenario but would do what I asked. I warned him to be careful if he went out of the building, to keep his eyes open for any unusual people hanging around. He scoffed and said, "This is New Haven, dude, everyone's unusual," and hung up.

I went to look in on Jessika. She was sitting up in bed. She smiled at me but her face told me she had been crying since I left her.

"You're awake, good. We need to get you out of here. I'm going to take you to a friend's place, where you can be safe. That way, I can also have people I trust with you while I'm figuring this thing out."

She looked at me, a scared little puppy. I could see her gearing up to cry again. We couldn't afford the waterworks so I sat on the bed and took her by the shoulders.

"Look at me. You need to trust that I will protect you. I can't do it from here. I need to take you where I feel confident that you'll be looked after."

She nodded, then pulled herself together quickly, getting up and grabbing an oversized bag from her closet. She started throwing clothes and toiletries in it, enough for a few days. I had her get a scarf to wrap around her face. She found a Yankee cap to cover her head to make her vaguely unrecognizable and we were ready to travel.

I called for an Uber and we went downstairs to wait in the corridor until I got the text that it had arrived. I picked up her bag along with mine and moved her quickly out to the waiting car. I gave the driver the address for Reilly's and 20 minutes later we pulled up to his apartment complex. I had the driver pull into the rear parking lot, got out first, looked around until I was satisfied that no one was watching, then shuttled her out of the car and down the back staircase into the apartment. I had called Reilly from the car and he was waiting there to open the door.

His apartment had once been a convent. The bottom floor was a warren of rooms, the biggest one used as his bedroom. After a quick introduction, he showed her where to stash her stuff and told her to make herself comfortable, then to come upstairs when she was ready. He and I walked up the stairs to the main floor.

As soon as we got out of her earshot, he turned and started laying into me.

"What the hell can you possibly be thinking, bringing her here? You said you thought they were watching you. If that's true, you don't think they'll know who your friends are? How easy would it be to find out where I live? If these guys are who you think they are, doesn't it make sense that they would have all kinds of connections and access to unlimited resources? Are you out of your fuckin' mind? What..."

I put my hand up and raised my voice loud enough to stop him. "Hey! Whoever's doing this has ratcheted up the game. I can't bring her to my place, not after spotting the Caddy trolling outside. There's nowhere else to bring her that's even remotely safe. Coming here was the best I could come up with for right now."

He glared at me but knew I was right. I hoped that I was.

After a minute, Jessika came up the stairs and into the kitchen where we were standing. She seemed to have gathered herself together and was relatively calm. Reilly asked her if she wanted anything.

"Do you have any coffee? Could I maybe have some coffee?"

I looked at him and he looked back at me, then scowled, said, "Sure," then set about making her one. I wanted one myself but didn't want to push my luck.

"And I suppose you want an Americano?"

Ah, he'd read my mind, all was forgiven.

"Love one. Thanks."

I led Jessika over to the couch and we sat and didn't say anything for a few minutes. Then I started asking her some questions.

"Jess, I want you to think back and really concentrate. Do you have any idea at all who might be doing this? You know the people who own the Catwalk...is there any chance it might be one of those guys or somebody at work?"

The look on her face told me she hadn't thought about this as a possibility and this new line of questioning was scaring her anew. I changed my tactics.

"Hey, it might not be anyone from work. That would be a little obvious. It's gotta be a customer." I glanced at her to see if she was buying in to this. I wasn't sure so I continued asking questions.

"Do you have an issue with me going back to the club and digging deeper? I have questions I need to ask some of the staff, after I take a look at the video Tony gave me." I turned to Reilly and he pointed at the old VCR on the kitchen counter.

"Have it at, amigo. Not sure I remember how to hook it up but it can't be all that hard, so even you should be able to do it."

She looked over at the VCR and then back to me. "I don't mind but you must know that it's not going to be easy to get anything from those guys. They protect that place like it was a bank or something."

I nodded. "Hey, I can be charming and persuasive when I need to be. One more question. Do you know Anthony Delmonico?"

She sat straight up quickly and the color went out of her face, coupled with a look of terror.

"Why? Did somebody say something? I didn't say anything to anybody." Tears again.

I put my hand on her arm to steady her. She jumped. "Jess, it's okay. I'm just curious. His name has come up a few times. Tell me what you know." She sat back and looked at me. It was going to take a while.

"Can I get some water?"

I looked over at Reilly and he rolled his eyes, grabbed a glass down from the cupboard, let the tap run, and filled it almost to the top. He reached his hand out with the glass in it and made me get up from the couch to go over and get it.

"Thanks for the effort, Chief."

He nodded, irked. I wasn't sure what was going on with him but whatever it was would have to wait until later. I handed Jessika the water and she took a big gulp, then started telling me the story.

"Anthony and I used to date. The first time I met him, I thought he was really good looking and seemed to be a gentleman. He came into the club one night while I was on stage and I noticed him right away. Everyone did. It seemed like a big deal, him being there. Everyone acted like he was somebody special and they all fell over trying to wait on him. I was impressed but didn't really think about it more than that. Then I noticed him watching me the whole time I was on stage. When I was done and getting down, he was there, waiting. He held out his hand and helped me down, introducing himself as the owner of the club. It surprised me, I thought Tony was the owner and said so. He shook his head, said it was him and that he thought I was the most beautiful dancer working there. I thought it was a line. I'd heard it a hundred times before, a hundred different ways. But he had this intensity, this way of looking at you that made you want to believe whatever he was telling you."

She took in a deep breath and took another swig of water before continuing.

"It was fun going out with him at first. He took me to really nice restaurants, here and in the city. We went to the Indian casino a few times. He'd give me a hundred dollars to play the slots and he'd play poker, you know, at the high roller tables. They all seemed to know him there. We would get the royal treatment and, I admit, it turned my head a little. People waiting on you, hand and foot? It jades you."

She looked off, remembering, then continued.

"Don't get me wrong, it wasn't only about the going

places and spending the money...in the beginning, he was very sweet and attentive. It didn't matter that he was older. He took his time, treated me like I was special. He would call me twice a day, just to say hello. It was nice."

She paused to catch her breath. She was trying hard to keep it together.

"After a few months, it started to change. He didn't call me as much. I only saw him once a week, if that. When we were together, we'd have sex and then he'd be distant, like he had no use for me. I was pretty sure it was going to be over soon, that it had just been a fling. Finally, he took me to Tre Scalini one night and told me over dessert that he didn't want to see me anymore, that he wanted to date other people. It hurt but I'd seen it coming and I was ready for it. He drove me home and I thought that was it, end of story."

Her breathing had become more erratic and her hands were shaking. Her face was flushed.

"I didn't see him for a while after that but a few months later he started showing up at the club again, watching me dance from his back table. He didn't talk to me, just sat and watched. It started to freak me out. I finally got up the nerve to go over and talk to him and ask him what was going on. He gave me a weird look and said he wanted to start up again. I told him that I wasn't interested and went back to the dressing room. He got up from his table and followed me in there. He was really mad and locked the door behind him."

The look on her face told me this was going to get unpleasant. I looked over at Reilly who was now hanging on every word. The disdain on his face had changed to anger as he saw where her story was going too.

"He threw me around a little. I screamed but nobody came. He slapped me, hard, and I fell down and hit my head on the coffee table that's there. I started bleeding and that must have scared him, because he stopped. He unlocked the door and left the club."

She lowered her head and I could see she was trying to keep from crying. I wasn't sure what to do here. I didn't want to touch her, wanting her to feel safe. Reilly felt no such compunction and came over, motioning for me to get off the couch, then sat down and put his arm around her shoulders. It sent her over the top and she cried violently for the next ten minutes, only interrupted by the front doorbell. Jessica sat upright and moved off the couch, ready to bolt. I stood up as well and moved in front of her. Reilly looked at us both standing, stood up himself, and moved towards the door.

"Relax, the two of you, it's just my sister. I called her to come over to help." He went out into the hallway and came back thirty seconds later, his sister Kathy behind him. He had evidently filled her in. She walked over to the couch, took Jessika's hand and sat down, pulling Jess down to sit with her. She shooed me away with her other hand. They looked at each other for a minute and then Kathy took her in her arms and hugged her, as if to never let her go. The look on her face told me it may have been the safest Jessika felt in quite some time.

I motioned for Reilly to follow me out of the room. We could hear her sobbing as we walked downstairs.

"I'm gonna go see if I can find this mutt. Can I leave her here for now?"

He agreed and I left her in the care of the Reillys. It was late and I had a rumbling in my stomach that made me realize I hadn't eaten since the bagel that morning. Walking back to my apartment, I tried to think about what my next steps would be but my mind was racing and nothing remotely coherent was coming to the forefront. I decided I needed to eat something if I was to continue being the protector of good against evil.

FOURTEEN

I walked down State and went up Crown Street, stopping in at Jake's Diggity Dogs. They were always open late and made great sausages and hot dogs. I opted for a Chicago-style dog, complete with tomato, green relish, onions, peppers, a pickle spear and celery salt. It was delicious and it took all the willpower I could muster not to get another. I would need a nap after and I didn't have the luxury of being able to do that. I finished it on the walk back to the apartment, using a Barq's root beer to wash it down.

Once inside my apartment, I booted up my ancient laptop again to see if I could find anything more on Anthony Delmonico.

There wasn't a lot that I hadn't already read about or heard from Mickey. Small-time hood who had a father in the New Haven mob. They used to hang out at a local restaurant, an old-school Italian joint with his namesake that had long gone out of business. In its heyday, Delmonico's had been considered "high-end" fancy, replete with stucco walls, Roman columns and off-the-boat waiters in black jackets, serving enormous plates of spaghetti and meatballs, eggplant parmesan and manicotti. This was long before you could only get the watered down, fake versions available from the myriad of chain Italian restaurants that were popular now.

I remembered going there in my late teens. It was an impressive place to bring a date. A little "spendy," as they say in the Midwest, but well worth it.

They had a private room (weirdly situated in the front of the restaurant) and, more often than not, you could glance in there when the door opened and see a bunch of guys that looked like the cast of *Goodfellas*. Waiters would constantly be bringing enormous plates of food in and taking back empty ones.

The bar was on the other side of the restaurant, separated by a half wall from the dining area. Again, depending on where you had been seated, one could watch as expensive bottle after bottle went in to that private room, wine and harder stuff, followed later on by the requisite Sambuca, cannoli, and many, many tiny cups of espressos.

You always got the impression that those guys would be sitting in the same place long after the place closed and everyone had left. All the patrons seemed to know who they were and everyone deferred to them. I once watched a guy who had been waiting in line for the men's room give up a stall to one of the guys from the back room, even though he was next and the line was long. It was a form of respect that I was unaccustomed to.

I didn't live in New Haven in those days. My foster family owned a small cape in Hamden and I went to high school there. Once I could drive, though, I was in New Haven often. There were clubs and concerts and restaurants. It was a little dangerous and exciting. The murder rate was high and you took your life in your hands walking in certain areas of the city.

Except for Wooster Street.

Known as "Little Italy," this was the Italian section of New Haven, famous for pizza, cherry blossoms and Italian restaurants. It was also home to many of the connected guys, members of the mob who had lived there for generations.

Originally, it was an area where many of the ship captains who sailed out of New Haven Harbor had lived. Wealthier citizens built gorgeous Victorian homes and lived there until the end of the 1800s, when a large number of Italian immigrant families settled there in response to an increased industrial activity in the area. The section started to lose its luster and plans were made to run I-91 through it. There were protests, and a movement to save the area for its historical aspects succeeded in making the city revitalize Wooster Square. This was in the 1930's.

A few years after that, a number of "made" guys from New York began to claim New Haven for their own. Guys with big reputations like Ralph Tropiano of Murder Inc., Billy Grasso and, most famously, Midge Renault. All were from high profile crime families like Gambino and Genovese. These guys trafficked in bootleg liquor, gambling and numbers, protection and much more. Eventually, the infighting and gang wars between the families began to rage and took its toll. The state cracked down on them and the organizations fell apart. Many left New Haven and went back to New York.

There were always some stragglers. Over the years, as the city gentrified and progress changed the need for the "services" these guys rendered, their power waned until it was almost non-existent. But they were still going strong in the 1970's and 80's.

When these guys weren't in the restaurants or the pizza places, they tended to hang out in these little storefronts they'd call "social clubs." Invitation only. The younger wannabe gangsters would have to "do penance" there, serving the "made" guys espressos and running errands.

Anthony grew up in one of those places. He started doing small things for his dad, like running numbers. Also known as the Italian lottery, this was an illegal betting game that almost everyone played every day. And while the game was run in other neighborhoods with all the other nationalities, the Italians made it into an art form.

There was one social club that was a little more famous that the others: Santa Anna Dominica.

I decided I would go there, first thing tomorrow.

FIFTEEN

My initial thought the next morning was that, before I headed out on this crazy new mission, I needed to see a friendly face, or, at the very least, hear a friendly voice. A beautiful face and voice. I called Reilly first to check in and we agreed to meet later at Trinity. Right after I hung up from him, I called Rosalind, the nurse I had been seeing for a few months. She answered on the second ring.

"As I live and breathe, if it isn't Tommy Shore!" She wasn't Irish but she liked to affect a little brogue every now and again. It made me smile.

"Hey, c'mon, it hasn't been that long, has it?" I couldn't actually remember when we last spoke or went out.

"Well, long enough for a gal to start having second thoughts..." She was having me on, or at least I thought she was. I was sure of it when I heard her laugh gently.

"I'm teasing. I missed you. What have you been up to?"

I weighed how much I wanted to tell her. Less is more sometimes.

"Been on a case, busy. Stalker deal. Trying to find out who's doing it and trying to put a stop to it. Unusual crowd of people on this one."

She laughed again. "Unusual? That's saying something for you. The folks that you get involved with always tend towards the more...unusual...side."

I decided to change the subject. "How about I make it up to you and take you out to dinner? There's a new hotel in New Haven called the Blake and they have a terrific restaurant there. I know the people running it. Are you on call Friday?"

She was an ER nurse at Yale-New Haven and when she wasn't on a shift, she needed to be available on call to go in if needed.

"You're in luck, boy-o! I just happen to be off this weekend, with no real plans except for reading and relaxing. Which day and what time?"

I loved her take-charge attitude. "How about 7:00 for drinks Friday and I'll make an 8:00 for dinner? The Blake has a rooftop bar that's on the youngish side, but the restaurant bar is nice. The restaurant, Hamilton's, is very good. Let's meet there?"

We agreed, shared a few more pleasantries, and then hung up. I felt a lightness I hadn't felt in a few days. My stepmother had always said that it was good to have something to look forward to and it was one of the few things she was ever right about. I called the restaurant and made a reservation.

I was still thirsty from last night's hot dog. I grabbed a Topo Chico out of the fridge, using the counter as a bottle opener. I had discovered the stuff during one of the few times I had ventured into Whole Foods. They had been sampling small cups of the stuff and I was immediately addicted. The effervescent mineral water cooled me down immediately.

I took out a legal pad and started jotting down the facts as I knew them so far. Looking over my notes confirmed that the social club was my best bet for watching Delmonico until I had a better plan. Surveillance was going to be my first order of business so I needed a car, one that I could sit in for long periods of time on Wooster Street and not garner much attention. I called the Hertz place I used regularly and asked for a plain, black sedan, finally settling on a Hyundai Elantra, evidently the car of choice for people not wanting to be noticed.

I grabbed my wallet, the rest of my drink and my sap off the table next to the door, locked up the apartment and went out the side door.

I walked down College to George Street, turned left and walked down to State. The Hertz dealer had the car ready and I was on the road in less than 20 minutes.

I drove across State and jockeyed the vehicle around the side streets until I hit Olive Street and then Wooster. Driving slowly, I cruised the block, passing Sally's Apizza on one side and a closed-up comedy club on the other. It had only lasted a year or so before turning into a biker bar, then ultimately shuttered. I was wistful, as that had been the location of the original Delmonico's restaurant.

I cruised by the apartment buildings that were built in the 1950s and never changed, then slowly past the La Bella Vita liquor store, another Italian restaurant, the famous Frank Pepe's Apizza, an Italian pastry store and another pizza shop. I finally spotted an open space that was across the street from that joint and almost directly across from Tony's "club." Yet another new pizza place had just recently opened and a space was open right in front of it.

The building the club was in was completely nondescript. It looked like it could be a bodega or a place where the Elks Club met. The only indication that there was more going on inside was the guy sitting outside, balancing himself on a small folding chair in front of the door. He was smoking a cigarette and looked like he'd come right out of central casting to be in the next Scorsese movie. Leather jacket with a wife-beater t-shirt underneath; dark black hair, worn slicked back; shiny brown pants that looked like they went with an outdated sharkskin suit; and pointy shoes in highly polished black patent leather. A sartorial amalgam of some-body's idea of a small-time hood. He was chewing on a toothpick. I decided to call him "Vinnie," to complete the stereotype.

I sat and watched him for a half hour. I wasn't sure what I was waiting to see. I knew I wanted to get a good look at Delmonico and possibly see if there was any kind of pattern to his frequenting the club but, other than Vinnie, there didn't seem to be anyone else going in or out.

I looked around at the rest of the street. There had been some early birds going into some of the pizza joints but the street, for the most part, was relatively quiet. It started me thinking back to a time when the area thrived, when there were always throngs of people here.

Every year, the city held a festival called the Avest, to celebrate the Feast of St. Andrew.

They would close down Wooster Street, the entire length of it, and vendors would set up stands. Sausage and peppers, fried dough slathered with tomato sauce and parmesan, calzones, freshly made candied apples and pastries, and, of course, pizza. Hundreds of people would crowd the streets, eating, drinking and enjoying themselves. It went on for days and people prepared for it for months.

There would be a daily parade that went down Wooster Street, replete with a statue of the saint, and people would attach single dollar bills to it. At the end of the fest, thousands would be collected. Within a mile of Wooster Square, there were at least a dozen Catholic churches that would get a piece of the action.

My reverie was interrupted by a movement toward the car. I turned and saw Vinnie walking over to me. I hit the button to let the window down.

He nodded his chin up to me once and asked, "Yo, whattya doin' here?" There wasn't a lot of malice in his voice but enough to let me know that he expected an answer. So much for my un-noticeable car.

I chuckled at his accent. He sounded like Johnny-boy from "Mean Streets." I wasn't sure if it was put-on or real. He was all in with the image.

"Napping."

He visibly scoffed. "Yeah, right. You been here a while. Kinda making me nervous."

I looked at him a few seconds and asked, "And you are...?"

He looked confused. "Whattya mean?"

I smiled again. "Who are you and why do you care

what I'm doing here?" The best defense is always a strong offense.

He visibly stiffened, then got aggressive. "Never mind who I am, I asked you who you were."

I considered it for a few seconds then decided I would lay it all out, see where it took me.

"Name's Tommy Shore. I'm looking to have a conversation with Anthony Delmonico."

I could see he was slightly taken aback by that answer and had been ready to start something up if I refused to give him something satisfying. I could see him struggling with what to do next.

"He in there?" I asked, pointing my chin towards the club.

He turned and looked at the door, in case I was talking about something else, then turned back and said, "I'll see if he wants to meet you." He walked away and went inside, looking back at me a couple of times. A few minutes went by before he came back out.

"Anthony says for you to come inside."

I looked at him, deciding on whether I wanted to take the chance. After I had said I wanted to meet Delmonico, I realized I would be on my own, with no idea how many guys were in there.

I opened the car door, got out and crossed the street with him. He stopped and motioned for me to raise my arms so he could pat me down. I laughed.

"Really?"

He nodded. "Can't be too careful these days."

I wanted to ask him some questions but it was already getting weird so I lifted my arms and said, "Take me to your leader."

I got the confused look again. "Huh?"

"Lead the way."

I heard him cluck his tongue, finished patting me down for a gun, then opened the door to take me inside. I was happy I left the sap in the glove box.

It occurred to me that I had no backup plan. Oh well, like my stepmom used to say, in for a penny, in for a pound.

And hopefully not a pound of flesh.

SIXTEEN

I followed Vinnie through the front door of the club. It was dark inside and it took a few minutes for my eyes to adjust. I was aware of two younger guys sitting at a small table to my immediate left and another guy standing on my right, behind a small makeshift bar. He was pouring drinks from one of the bottles sitting on top of the bar. It was still early in the day but I wanted a shot of Jameson to help with the dry mouth I was experiencing. Although it was doubtful that they would have that here...probably just Sambuca and Frangelico.

As my focus returned, I could see a guy I figured to be Delmonico sitting at a table in the back, with another guy sitting to his left. The other guy was huge and brawny, probably a bodyguard. Delmonico's Luca Brasi or some such nonsense. Vinnie led me back there.

I was right about which one was Delmonico. He was a good-looking guy but fading fast. In his mid-40s or so, he was small with a slight build. I figured 5'9" or so. His hair was slicked back and loaded up with some kind of gel. He was beginning to go bald so it looked thin on top. My guess was that the gel was supposed to thicken it up but it failed miserably. He had on a black shirt and was wearing a slightly darker black tie. And jeans. I could see a black jacket hanging on a coat rack slightly behind him and to his right. Gangster chic. He didn't look up from the paper he was reading.

There was an open chair at the table and the big guy gestured for me to sit in it. I nodded and took the seat. The big guy got up and walked away, heading out a door I figured led to a kitchen.

After thirty seconds or so, Delmonico finally looked up. "Would you like an espresso?" asked at the same time as nodding to one of the younger guys that had been on my left when I entered. The nearer of the two got up immediately and went over to an espresso machine near the makeshift bar and started making the coffees. I smiled, shrugged and said, "Sure. Black."

He returned the smile, tight-lipped and cocksure. I half expected him to ask me if he amused me. The whole place felt like a movie fantasy being played out.

"Of course. Is there any other way?" I shrugged and nodded again. It was turning out to be my master plan.

The kid who had been making the coffees came over, put his boss's cup down in front of him first, waited for a nod of approval, and then placed mine in front of me. Delmonico kept watching me, then folded up the newspaper and asked me, "So, what can I do for you? Bobby tells me you've been sitting outside and watching the club for a while and that you want to speak with me. What can I help you with?"

Evidently, Vinnie was actually Bobby.

He was working hard to come across as intelligent, making sure he enunciated each word properly, aware of the stereotype. I respected that and decided to lay it all out on the table.

"A few days ago I met a woman who dances at the Catwalk. Her name is Jessika but she dances under the nom de plume of Candy. She'd received some threatening messages from someone who was stalking her. As you can imagine, this upset her. She asked me to look into the threats and, if possible, to find the person responsible. Once I did that, I was to find a way to make that person cease and desist. I started looking into the club to see if I could determine anything from there and that led me to you. I know you own the Catwalk. I also know you and Jessika were an item for a while. I wanted to get a sense of who I was dealing with so I decided to take a look at this place, put a face to a name. That's when Bobby spotted me and came over to the car. I decided it was an opportunity for us to meet. And here we are."

I watched his face as he took in what I was telling him. His expression hadn't changed the entire time I was talking. Must be a good poker player. He looked like he was trying to decide how much of threat I was to him. A solid thirty seconds went by.

"Tommy...hopefully, I can call you Tommy... Tommy...I applaud your diligence. It's not an easy discovery that the Catwalk is mine. You must have had to dig down deep to find that out."

I nodded at the compliment and remembered Jessika had mentioned his intensity. She was spot on there. I kept quiet and he continued.

"I do know Jessika and, yes, we did see each other for a while. She's a lovely girl. Maybe a touch high strung but I chalked that up to our difference in ages. I liked being with her and, I admit, I liked the attention I got when she was on my arm. I took her to New York and a number of high-end places. We always had a good time."

He stopped to sip his espresso so I sipped mine, keeping my eyes on him the entire time. I was aware Bobby was still inside and sitting close by. He seemed to be occupied elsewhere but I got the feeling he was listening to every word. Delmonico continued talking.

"I have a number of businesses and a few of them started to need extra attention. I'm afraid I didn't spend as much time with her as I probably should have and didn't pay her enough attention. Girls like that need constant attention. I didn't have the time and so I broke it off."

The story he was laying out so far seemed to line up with the one Jessika had told me. I was waiting for the part where it went wrong.

"A few months later, I found myself missing her. I went to the club to watch her dance and realized I still had feelings for her. I was surprised when she approached me and asked me if I wanted to get involved again. I told her I thought that I might and that maybe we could go out for dinner some evening. We had dinner a few times where afterwards, she spent the night at my home, but I eventually realized that we really had nothing in common and that I was no longer interested. She didn't take it well. There was some yelling and name calling. I had one of my guys, Bobby, drive her home. I thought that would be the end of it. Later, I discovered that some things were missing from my home, things with monetary value but more importantly, things with sentimental value. A gold Rolex that my late father had left me and an opal ring my mother used to wear. I wasn't entirely sure she had taken them. There are a number of people coming into my home, housekeepers and cooks and the like. It certainly could have been any of those people...but Jessika had the most access to my bedroom where I kept those things and she certainly had the opportunity. I sent Bobby over to speak with her but she denied having taken them. I decided to let it go and that's the last I've seen or spoken about her. Until now."

I tried to keep my feelings off my face. This was a very different story from the one Jessika had told me. Delmonico had relayed it without much emotion and it had the effect of making me believe it might be true. The part I didn't believe was that he would "let it go." If he was telling me the truth, it meant that Jessika had been lying to me. I tried to keep my anger in check until I spoke with her and made a mental note to look around her apartment more carefully the next time I was there. All I wanted now was to get out of this place and find her.

"Well, Anthony...can I call you Anthony? I truly appreciate your taking the time to see me. It's certainly been enlightening. I'm going to continue my search for whoever's been threatening Jessika but I feel comfortable ruling you out."

One of the first things you're told when you start learning to play poker is to never tip your hand. I wanted Delmonico at ease and accepting that I believed him, that I had gotten what I'd come for.

I stood up and was aware that Luca had come back into the room. All five guys were watching me to see if there was still a threat. I put out my hand to Delmonico.

He paused a few seconds then took it by the tips of my fingers. Pope-like. I resisted calling him "Your Holiness" and walked out the door, crossing the street to my car. I didn't look back.

There was a parking ticket on the windshield. I looked around but couldn't see the meter maid. I chalked it up to the cost of doing business in this part of town. I headed over to Trinity. Nothing like a few Jamesons to take a bad taste out of your mouth.

SEVENTEEN

When I got to Trinity, Reilly was already there, watching the Liverpool game and deep into his Guinness. Trinity was a great bar that he and I had been going to more often, ever since the Owl had started getting too fufu, with overpriced drinks and bartenders wearing uniforms. Trying too hard to be New York instead of New Haven...and failing miserably.

Trinity bar, on the other hand, was a great Irish pub with reasonably priced pours of fine Irish whiskey and Guinness on tap. The staff was very friendly and always accommodating, many of them Irish. Richie, the head bartender, was a Class A ballbreaker in a good way, and we could banter back and forth with him throughout the night. He loved jokes and always had a one-liner to share as soon as I walked in.

"Tommy! You're here. Finally! Hey, you know the worst time to have a heart attack? During a game of charades! What'll ya have?"

I groaned and laughed and asked for the usual, but

he'd already grabbed the bottle of Jameson and a glass and had begun pouring me one.

The place was full, typical for that time of the day. I moved down the full bar to the end, where Reilly was standing and watching a 70-inch screen that was fastened to the back wall, with a projector box showing the soccer channel. They televised all of the games here, at all hours of the day. With a decent breakfast and cheap but tasty wings and nachos, the place was always hopping.

Reilly was yelling at the screen. Liverpool was down a goal and he evidently felt the players could hear him screaming at them and would pick up their play. I put my hand on his shoulder and he looked over, smiled a tight, wry smile, and said, "Yo, Charlie Chan, what's shakin'?"

I shook my head at the dated reference, once again from some distant corner of the recesses of his brain. "Aren't there any detective references you can use that are from, say, the last ten years? Maybe one that relates to the right race?"

He snarled at me, said "Liverpool is losing," and handed me his empty beer glass. Years of drinking together told me that meant he needed another. I went back to the bar and Richie pulled a Guinness from the tap, bellowing, "Reilly's a thirsty one today, eh?" I nodded, saying, "And that's different how?" He laughed and I took the beer over. He had relocated to a high-top table along the wall where it was slightly quieter and we could talk. He got right to the point.

"So, where are we with the stripper? Have you figured out what we're gonna do?"

I smiled at the use of the royal "we" and laid out all

the details of my Wooster Street adventure. He listened intently, without any discernible reaction, but when I was done, he chugged down the remainder of his beer, stood up and started putting his coat on. It confused me.

"Are we leaving?"

He shot me a look like I'd asked him if the earth was round, and shook his head.

"You poked the bear, Kemosabe. You don't think there's gonna be retaliation? We need to get back to my place, figure out the next move and check in on your stripper."

I shot him a glance. "Stop calling her that. She's an exotic dancer." I was sorry I said it as soon as the words left my mouth. He laughed, but with a meanness that I hadn't heard from him before.

"Listen, Hoss, give it a name. Whichever way you want to refer to her choice of occupation is fine by me but you're gonna get this girl hurt or killed. I understand that you believe these guys no longer run things around here anymore...but that doesn't mean that they believe it. And if they think they can still do whatever the hell they want to do, it's a solid bet they will. So, let's get outta here and make sure everything is still cool at my place."

I nodded, having lost the will to argue with him anymore.

We walked out the front door and turned to walk towards Chapel Street. He crossed the street against the light, and I followed. About halfway down the block, he stopped and turned to me. "I need smokes and lotto tickets. Be right out," and he went into the small bodega there. So much for urgency.

When he came out, we continued walking down Chapel to Wooster Park and over to his apartment. As we went inside, we could both tell something was wrong. The apartment was dark and we stopped to listen for movement or voices, possibly downstairs on the lower level. We heard nothing.

Reilly called out, "Hey, you guys downstairs?" but there was no answer. We both went down the narrow staircase, with Reilly going through one set of doors that led one way and me through the other. The bedroom was joined on two sides by a bathroom and we reached that area together. He looked at me and shook his head. I was going to suggest we go back upstairs and try to call Kathy's cell when mine rang. It was Jessika, calling on Kathy's phone.

"Tommy, we're in Kathy's car, driving to Victor's apartment. I didn't know where else to go. I'm scared. There were phone calls and I..." She was crying again.

I tried to calm her. "Jess, take a deep breath. Can you put Kathy on the phone?"

I heard the phone being shuffled and Kathy got on. Her voice was clipped as she said, "Tom. She's safe but I wanted to get her out of there. Her cell phone kept ringing with no one on the other end and no caller ID. I didn't want to take a chance that whoever might be looking for her might be able to track where she is. We left her phone in the apartment. She suggested going to Victor's."

I didn't want them to go there. "No, that's not gonna work. Whoever's doing this probably knows about her friendship with Victor. My place is out, too. I've seen some suspicious cars around there lately."

I tried to think of a safe place to take her. Nothing

came to mind until I hit upon an old friend who lived in West Haven. I would need to check with him first to see if it was okay.

"Listen, find a place to pull over and wait for me to call back, a McDonald's or a Dunkin' Donuts, someplace fairly well lit up. Don't go in though and park away from the entrance. Try to find a spot where you can watch the other cars coming in. I've got to make a phone call and see if I can find you a safe spot."

She agreed and hung up. Reilly had been patiently waiting for me to get off the phone so I told him the story then dialed my friend.

Michael had been a top executive with one of the biggest record companies in the world. We had been friends since high school, when he lived around the corner from my foster home. He'd had a stellar position in A&R, signing a number of acts over a 23-year career that had become very successful. But a battle with his personal demons caused him to walk away from it all and he came back to Connecticut to downsize his life. He had put together a private label and was working hard to break new acts in a business that had taken a lot of hits over the years. As each of us pursued our various careers, we had drifted apart. Now he was living in a rented house that had been converted to a recording studio and he reached out to me a few years back. We reconnected. Since he was a hardcore cigar smoker, we would meet occasionally for a coffee and a smoke, and to reminisce. I trusted him.

He picked up on the third ring. "Michael, it's Tommy."

"Hey, pal, whattya need?" I knew he conducted

much of his business on his cell so phone conversations needed to be terse.

"I need to put a friend up at your house for a few days. I can't explain everything right now but she's hiding out and I need a place that nobody knows about. I thought you could help me out."

He didn't hesitate. "Of course. Is she hot?"

I laughed. He was a notorious skirt chaser in his day, but with a penchant for black women.

"She is but not really in your particular wheel-house, amigo."

He chuckled loudly. "Oh, okay, so she's white?" He laughed again.

I needed to get back to Kathy. "Look, I'm going to send her over now. She's being driven by another friend. Her name is Kathy. It's gotta be done quietly, understood? I'll tell her to pull all the way in to the rear of the house so you can take her up the back staircase, yes?"

"Sure, sure. Jesus, what'd this girl do? Piss off some gangster?"

The question startled me but I composed myself. "You're close. I'll tell you later when I come to get her. I really appreciate this."

He laughed again, said "No worries," and hung up. I called Kathy back and gave her directions to the place and what to do once they got there. She didn't argue. Some traits don't pass from brother to sister. Thankfully.

EIGHTEEN

Reilly and I got into the rental and headed towards West Haven. He was unusually quiet for most of the ride, which usually meant one of two things – he was either very tired or he was pissed off. Might be both. I decided to speak first.

"What's going on with you? You okay?"

He kept looking out of the window and took a while to answer.

"Not really. I still can't find a doctor that'll tell me conclusively what these episodes I've been having are. I'm tired all the time. I can barely work. Just want to sleep."

My first thought was the booze couldn't be helping. I didn't want to say it, though...the last thing he needed was another mother. I decided to try a psychological route.

"Hey, maybe we need to cut back on the Jameson and Guinness? That can't be helping. I've been feeling it myself lately."

He finally looked over at me and scoffed, saying

sarcastically, "Right, 'we' stop drinking and that'll make everything right with the world. Give me a break. And don't use that psych 101 shite on me."

I knew as I said it that it wouldn't fly and decided to just clam up. We didn't say another word for the rest of the ride.

We got to Michael's place in twenty minutes. It was on a central street, set back away from the curb. It was a three-level house in desperate need of major repair. The studio was at the back of the house in a free-standing building. The driveway entrance off the street curved around to a small lot that could accommodate parking for another three to four cars. Kathy's Subaru was there, easily recognizable by the BACK OFF, YA FECKIN' GOBSHITE! bumper sticker.

We entered the house from the back porch, walking up an old staircase to the second floor. I knocked softly on the door and Michael answered immediately.

"They're in the studio. Follow me."

He took us back down the stairs and across the driveway to the back of the other building. There was a small door with a buzzer that had to be pushed to be let in, but I'd never seen the door locked. I rang it anyway, then entered into the front room, a small kitchen. Vince, who owned the house and the studio, was sitting at the small kitchen table and spoke directly to Michael in a whisper.

"Are these the guys? 'Bout time. Where'd they come from, Peru?"

I looked at Reilly, who shrugged, then bulled his way past, yelling out for Kathy as he went in.

I followed. Kathy came out from another room and spoke to me first.

"Thank god you're here. She's a basket case. The constant cellphone ringing with nobody there put her over the top. She's in the recording studio."

I nodded, thanked her, and went past, down a long corridor that ran the length of the building and led into a control booth. I could see her through the glass, sitting on a chair in the recording area, behind a bevy of microphones and cables. She was holding her head and crying softly. I went through another door and into the studio. Her crying intensified when she saw me. I put my arm around her and tried to calm her, saying it would be okay and that I would protect her, wondering if the words sounded as hollow to her as they did to me.

She looked up at me, the pain all over her face. "What am I going to do? Anthony's going to kill me."

I shook my head. "I'm not going to let that happen. And we don't know that it's him yet. Yes, he is the top suspect but I have no proof yet that he did any of this. We met today."

Her eyes got wide. "You met him? Where? What did he say? Is he mad?"

"Well, he told me a slightly different story from the one you told me. He said that you approached him when he came back to the club, that it was your idea to get involved again. He said that he realized after a few dates that he was no longer interested and called it off. But he also said that some things were missing from his house, things with sentimental value. Any of this true?"

She looked away from me, avoiding my eyes. I realized I'd hit a nerve and that, true to form, the truth was somewhere in between the two stories. Her breathing had returned to normal and the waterworks had stopped. When she looked back at me, it was a very different Jessika. Harder.

"It sorta is. But what I told you wasn't a total lie. He did come back to see me at the club but he didn't come back to my dressing room and start throwing me around like I told you. I made that up to make sure you would keep helping me. I didn't know what else to do. We went out a few times after that. I spent a few nights at his place. But then he called it off. Said he didn't feel the same way about me anymore. I was really hurt, Tommy...but I didn't take anything from him, I swear I didn't!"

I looked at her, trying to get a glimpse of something that would help me believe her story...but I was troubled by what she hadn't said. She didn't ask me what items Delmonico claimed were missing and she didn't volunteer any information as to why she would have started up with him again. I wasn't really buying that she needed the roughing up story in order to get me to stay on the case. While it certainly would have done the trick, she didn't really know me well enough to use my "white knight" syndrome to get me to believe her story about him. I needed to think it through and figure out my next steps. I handed her back her cell phone, which I had brought with me from Reilly's.

"Listen, I'm going to ask my friend if you can stay here for a few days. Nobody knows about this place so you'll be safe, but you need to keep a low profile. I can't stress that enough. Which includes staying off your cell phone. Turn it off. When are you supposed to dance again?"

She considered the question, then opened her bag and pulled out a date book. She quickly checked the calendar and said, "No, I'm off for the next two days. Think I can smoke in here?" She reached in again and pulled a pack of cigarettes out of her seemingly bottom-less bag.

I looked around and saw a number of half-full ashtrays that looked like they'd hadn't been emptied in a while. The rest of the room was an amalgam of empty soda cans, fast food wrappers, and half bottles of liquor, magazines and sound equipment. For the first time, I noticed a musty, stale smell of sweat, body odor and unrealized ambition. I told her I thought she could but she had already lit one up before I finished the sentence.

"I'll be right back."

I went back outside, over to the house and back upstairs. Michael was sitting at his breakfast table, drinking a ginger ale. It looked like Reilly and Kathy had left. He looked up and smiled.

"Hey there. Your friend said to tell you that they needed to leave, that he wasn't feeling that good and that his sister would drive him home. He said you'd understand and to call him later. Everything okay over there? She seemed pretty upset."

I nodded, distracted. "She'll be fine. I just need some time to figure this out. Getting conflicting stories about what happened and why. She's on the run from some iffy characters and I'm out of safe places to hide her. Can she stay here for a few days? No one who knows me knows about you or this place so I'm pretty sure she'll be okay here."

He smiled at "pretty sure."

"Sure. I have an extra room. I'll talk to Vince and let him know she'll be staying here. I'll need to straighten things out a bit but she'll be comfortable. I'm in New York tomorrow but he can look in on her. Give me a few bucks so I can bring in food and whatever else she needs. Two days?"

I shrugged. "Shouldn't be much more than that. If it is, I'll find another place." I took out five twenties and handed them to him. "That should cover any food she needs and anything else. Might have to get her some cigs. It's okay if she smokes there?"

He laughed. "Vince smokes like a chimney, as does pretty much every band who comes in here to record, so yeah, it's fine. By the way, no one is scheduled for the rest of the week so you don't have to worry about strangers in the house."

I thanked him and walked back downstairs and into the studio. Jessika was where I left her, holding her face in her hands again. I walked over and touched her shoulder. She looked up slowly.

"You believe me, don't you?"

I nodded yes, that I did but I wasn't really sure, still skeptical about the entire thing. I figured there were at least three sides to this little drama and that the truth was firmly lodged somewhere in between. I changed the subject.

"Listen, stay here for a couple of days, up in the house. Read a book, watch TV, listen to music. Michael will take care of you. I gave him money for food and cigs and anything else you might need. But you need to promise me that you'll stay inside until I tell you otherwise. And remember what I said about your phone. I can't protect you if anyone knows where you are. Understood?"

She pouted a little but nodded that she got it. I

helped her stand up and led her out to the studio kitchen, where Michael had come down was waiting to show her the way upstairs to her room.

It didn't enter my mind that it would be the last time I would see her alive.

NINETEEN

I drove slowly back to New Haven, using the side streets. I wanted some extra time to review how things stood to try and formulate a plan. I wasn't sure who I believed, my client or her possible stalker. Both stories had an element of truth to them and my gut feeling was that neither of them would tell me what really happened.

I called Reilly to meet me back at Trinity. I was hungry and the food there was basic but good. He picked up immediately and said he would meet me, but I sensed a hesitation on his part. I wondered if getting Kathy involved shook him up a little. He was already nervous about these guys to begin with.

I found a space in front of the bar, unheard of for that time of day. I pulled in, parked and was starting to open the car door to get out and go in, when I heard a man's voice coming from outside the car on the passenger side.

"Get your ass back in the car and unlock this door." It was a command rather than a request. I thought I recognized the voice but couldn't be sure. I looked out the passenger window to see if I could identify who was talking but all I could see was the middle of his body, with a hand in his right jacket pocket, bulging slightly to signify he had a gun in there. I hit the unlock button.

Bobby, the guy who had been guarding Delmonico's club, got in.

"Drive!" He barked, like it was something he'd seen in the movies. I didn't respond. He grimaced and raised his voice. "Didn't you hear me, asshole? I said, drive!" He moved his hand around in his pocket some more.

I looked at him and said, "Such a prime space, I kinda hate to give it up." Then smiled wide.

It pissed him off and he started yelling. "You think this is a joke? What, I don't have a piece in here!?" He pulled his hand out of his pocket, bringing with it a small .38. I looked at it and stopped smiling. He actually grunted.

"What, no jokes now, funny guy? Drive!" he said, waving the gun towards the front window.

I weighed my options but there didn't seem to be any. I pulled out of the space and headed down Orange Street, turning left down Chapel, hoping that I might see Reilly walking towards the bar and maybe signal him somehow. No such luck.

"Where to?"

He glared at me. "Just drive. Take a left at State!" He was clearly agitated and said it through clenched teeth. I wasn't sure what might set him off so I treaded lightly. I drove down State Street for a half mile or so when he said, "Pull in here," indicating a driveway to a new restaurant, Nolo, that had opened there a few months back. It had been the location of Jet Cleaners forever but the new owners had converted it into a great dining space. I went once. It was okay. Hard for a new pizza joint to compete in this town.

Bobby used the gun to indicate that I was to go as far back into the lot as possible. The way in was also the way out so there wasn't any chance of my backing out onto the street without turning the car around. I pulled into a space near a fence, between two cars, far away from the entrance. When I turned towards him, he had the gun in his left hand and brought it around quickly across the side of my face. I was able to bring up my arm in time to soften the blow a bit but it still connected hard with my cheek. I couldn't see out of my right eye and it took me a minute to focus, waiting for another shot. I hadn't heard anything crack but knew that the first hit would leave a nasty bruise. I leaned back as far as I could and waited for his next move.

"You need to drop this thing you're doing with Jessika. She's off limits. She'll be fine. We'll take care of it. Got that?"

My face was throbbing from the blow and his voice seemed far away. I wasn't sure there wouldn't be more and tried to keep track of his movements with the eye that I could still see out of. He seemed to have calmed down a bit after he got that first bit of violence out of his system and it was a good thirty seconds before he spoke again.

"Consider this a warning. Walk away from Jessika. Next time, it's worse. Much worse." He got out of the car and I struggled to watch him as he walked back to another row of cars, got in one, and drove off. I couldn't see what the make was but it looked large. Like a Cadillac.

I realized this wasn't a spur of the moment thing. The whole thing had been planned.

I could feel my face start to swell and knew it would get worse quickly if I didn't get some ice on it. I got out, stumbled my way across the lot, and went into the restaurant. A young lady working the check-in desk looked at me and gasped.

"Oh my god, what happened?"

I looked at her and could see she was truly upset. It must look worse than I first thought.

"I fell in the parking lot and hit a car door handle on the way down. Do you think you could get me some ice wrapped in a towel?"

She ran off to the kitchen and I sat down on a bench in the waiting area. It was loud in there so nobody paid me much attention. The throbbing had escalated and I felt the pangs of a nasty headache coming on. The smells coming from the kitchen were having an adverse effect and I tried to fight back the nausea.

The hostess returned quickly and handed me a large towel, wrapped around a lot of ice. I pressed it to my face immediately. A young guy in a tie had come back with her and the two of them each took one of my elbows and guided me over to another sitting area, farther away from the front door.

I felt myself getting groggy and started to lean towards laying down on the bench but they both grabbed hold of my shoulders and started saying loudly that I should stay awake. I heard the young woman ask me if there was someone they could call. The last thing I told her before I passed out was Reilly's phone number.

TWENTY

I woke up on Reilly's couch, back at his apartment, with absolutely no idea how I'd gotten there or how long I'd been out. His sister Kathy was standing at the stove, cooking something, with the tea kettle on one of the back burners, whistling loudly that the water inside was boiling. She opened the lid on the spout and the whistling stopped. I watched her through a haze as she poured the water into a large mug and, within a few seconds, the aroma of the hot tea wafted over to where I was laying.

"Is that for me?" My throat was sore, and the words barely came out. She turned, saw I was awake, and brought the mug over to where I was, putting it down on the makeshift coffee table.

"Go slow, it's very hot, but try and drink as much of it as you can. It'll make you feel better. We can try something stronger in a little while."

I tried pulling myself up on my elbows, but the room started spinning. I laid back down quickly, groaning. She went back to what she was cooking on the stove.

"Seamus went out to get Tylenol and cigarettes. The staples of life here. You should just rest. He'll be back shortly."

After a few minutes, I tried again and was able to sit up with a minimal amount of room spin. The throbbing in my head refused to stop and I felt I might get nauseous again, but I closed my eyes and tried to focus on my breathing. After a few minutes had passed, it was almost tolerable. I reached for the tea and took a swig. It was still very hot, but the warmth felt good on my throat. I looked over at Kathy, who had finished cooking and was plating a small mound of scrambled eggs. She brought them over to me.

"You might not be able to get all of this down, but you should really eat something. You've been passed out for quite a while."

I turned to look out the big window, but it seemed dark out. I was having difficulty focusing my right eye but then remembered that Reilly liked to blacken the windows in this room so he could acclimate easier, usually after a bender.

I scanned the room again, trying to get my bearings. There was no television or clock. I wasn't sure where my phone was so I couldn't check the time. I took the eggs from Kathy and slowly tried to eat. My jaw was sore, and I felt every mouthful. She watched as I ate. She meant well but her staring was making me more irritable.

"What time is it? Have I been passed out all night?" It came out harsher than intended.

She started to answer but stopped when she heard

the keys to the front door of the apartment jangling. Reilly bounded in, carrying a small plastic bag from the bodega and a larger paper bag that clinked as he put it down on the kitchen island. Liquor supplies. He looked at the two of us, took it all in, and then started unpacking the bags. When he came to the Tylenol, he opened it up, shook three out into his hand, and brought them over to me.

"Here, take these." It wasn't a request.

I took the pills, popped them in my mouth, and picked up the tea to wash them down. I was never really a tea person and the taste made me grimace, which I immediately felt in my face. I winced again and Reilly scoffed.

"Jeez, that guy did a number on you. How many times did he hit you?"

The pain shot from my eye up to my head and I needed to look down to let it pass. When it subsided, I looked up at him and said, "Just once. I blocked it as much as I could but still caught the brunt of it. If I hadn't put my arm up, he might've broken my cheekbone."

He scoffed again. "He may have broken it anyway. Looks bad and turning all kinds of purple. Who did it?"

I couldn't keep my head up for more than a minute at a time. I used my hand to wave him off until I felt better, then laid back down and passed out again.

I awoke two hours later. When I sat up and looked around, Reilly was standing at one of his easels, painting. His art tended towards the semi-abstract but this painting looked to be about something. I could make out a landscape and some figures. I would need to wait for my vision to clear up before I took a closer look. I closed my eyes and laid back down.

Kathy must have left while I was out. My phone was now on the coffee table. I picked it up to look at the time. Almost noon. Reilly heard the movement and turned towards me.

"Back amongst the living, Hoss?"

I looked up and saw his face hovering above me, smiling widely. He bent over me, grabbed both my arms, and pulled me upright. I sat back, closed my eyes and tried to breathe.

"You're lucky you don't have a concussion. Wasn't sure we should've let you sleep but Kathy seemed to think it wasn't one, so I gave in. We also called your nurse friend, Rosalind, described what went on and she agreed. She said to call her when you're back on your feet."

I kept my eyes closed but nodded. He continued to talk.

"You know who did this, right? Was it the mob guy?"

I opened my eyes. My focus wasn't quite back yet. I tried to nod.

"It was a mob guy but not the one I've been watching. One of his guys. He warned me off the Jessika thing."

Reilly scowled. "Think the top guy sent him?"

I went over what happened in my head and remembered thinking that the short, one-sided conversation he'd had with me after he'd hit me felt unusual. He'd used her first name a few times. Not "the dancer" or "the stripper", or even "Candy". He had used Jessika.

Like he knew her or thought he knew her and had a relationship with her, even if only in his mind.

I shook my head. It hurt.

"I don't think so. The things this guy said to me were too familiar, too personal. I think he did this on his own. It was just him in the car. My limited knowledge of these bigshot mob guys is that they usually like to send two or more guys to make a point. This guy jacked me outside of Trinity. He knew I would be there, like he'd been watching our usual places. I also think the car he drove off in was a Caddy, like the one I saw outside my apartment. Can't be sure, my sight was blurred, but it looked like a big car."

Reilly stared at me for thirty seconds before he spoke. "So, you think this guy has a thing for her and went rogue? He'd be takin' a big chance, no, especially if the boss had a thing with her? If that's the case, we should probably figure out a plan of action before this guy finds out where we have her stashed."

I nodded but still couldn't think straight. There were too many questions coming up. I needed to get home and rest up before I could plan anything. I needed a hot shower and my own bed. I reached out for my phone and even that small effort took a toll. I was able to slide it over and dialed Michael's house. Jessika picked up. She answered on the first ring but waited for me to speak first.

"Hey there, it's Tommy. You okay?"

There was a hesitation before she answered.

"Yeah, I'm fine. Michael went out so I'm here alone. I've been watching some television and they got me some magazines. Mostly music stuff. I've tried to stay off my phone like you said but figured this might be you. Are you okay? Your voice sounds weird."

She had again regressed to being a small child. I could hear it in her voice. Scared but trying to put on a brave face. It made me realize that the time I had to deal with this thing would be limited before she would start to break down and do something stupid or crazy in order to get away from it all.

"No, I'm good. Sorry I didn't call you sooner, some stuff came up that I needed to handle."

I paused for more questions. When none came, I continued. "Jess, do you know a guy Bobby who works for Delmonico? Not sure of a last name. Medium build, black hair, likes to wear it slicked back?"

"That sounds like Bobby Trullo. He drives for Anthony. I kinda know him but not really. He drove me home a few times when Anthony didn't want me around. That guy?"

"Yeah, maybe. You never went out with him, right?

I could hear her scoff. "Are you kidding? He's so not my type. Thinks he's in *Goodfellas*. No, we had a few light conversations when he drove me home but nothing special. Why, did he say we had a thing?"

I didn't want this getting in her head. "No, no, I was just curious. Don't worry about it. I'm just trying to rule some stuff out. Listen, I gotta run but you hang tight, and I'll check in on you shortly. This should all be over soon. Promise."

She thanked me and we hung up. I looked at Reilly and motioned for him to give me a hand getting up. He helped me get to my feet. It took a minute to find my balance and once I did, I gathered my stuff and he drove me back to the lot to get the rental car. After making sure the city hadn't booted it, I drove home and found a space in the garage next door, on the first level above the street. Luckily. Any higher would have been an issue. I got out and gingerly made my way down the staircase and into my building.

Once in my apartment, I took a long shower, letting the hottest water I could stand ease the pain, then got dressed in sweats. I sat in my leather easy chair for a long while, thinking. There were a lot of loose ends here and getting them to form into a cohesive thought would take a while. The headache had receded enough to where I could maybe concentrate on a plan. I touched my face and recoiled at the soreness.

My cell phone rang, and I saw that it was Rosalind calling. I picked up on the second ring to a lovely laugh.

"Howdy, stranger. How are you holding up?"

It had only been a few days since we'd talked but she liked this greeting too and used it almost every other time we spoke, when she wasn't using her semi-passable Irish brogue.

"I'm okay. Kathy told me they called you and that they brought you up to speed on what happened. I'm fine. A little sore but I'll live. I was going to call you to tell you but needed a hot shower first. I was also going to tell you I need a raincheck for Friday."

I didn't feel much like going into details just yet and wanted to change the subject.

There was a hesitation on her end, until she finally said, "Okay, we can do it that way. I'm guessing you want some time to wrap your head around this? I can do the small talk thing. No worries about Friday. Just tell me you're really okay."

I wasn't sure if she was angry or not, but I wasn't up to a long, drawn-out conversation.

I took a deep breath and felt it in my cheek. The pain had lessened but it was still tender.

"Yeah, I'm really fine. I took the brunt of the hit with my arm, so nothing was broken, just bruised."

I let that float out there for a second then added, "Nothing that some TLC from a trained professional wouldn't cure."

It seemed to work. I could almost hear her smiling on the other end. There was a little more back and forth. I told her that we could shoot for Saturday instead, if she was still available. She said she understood, that I should call her whenever I got a chance and that we'd play it by ear, according to how I felt, then we hung up.

I sat in the chair a while longer, thinking about possible scenarios. I went back and forth in my head whether I should go see Delmonico first or deal with Trullo on my own. The former seemed to win the argument each time. These guys always gave a lot of lip service to "respect" and that would certainly be the respectful thing to do. Although I wasn't feeling all that respectful.

I eventually fell asleep. Any plans would have to wait.

TWENTY-ONE

It was a restless night, and I woke up late the next morning with a splitting headache. I laid in bed for a while, trying to orient myself, then forced myself to get up and begin trying to bring this particular nightmare to an end.

I had decided that I needed to confront Delmonico again, if only to confirm that he didn't send his monkey to warn me off, that Trullo had done it on his own. It was a risky chance to take but my gut told me it was the right move. The trick would be getting to him when he was alone. My best bet appeared to be when he was at the Catwalk.

Finding the numbers Jessika had written down for me, I called Victor's cell. He answered quickly.

"This is Victor."

"Victor, Tommy Shore. I need a favor."

He asked me to hold on a second. I could hear shuffling and thirty seconds later he was back on, whispering.

"I'm at work, doing inventory again. I don't have a lot of time. Can it wait until this afternoon?"

It wasn't the response I expected.

"Nice. How about, 'Hey Tommy, how's Jess?' That would be the proper response from someone who's supposed to be her friend." I wasn't in the mood for morons and couldn't keep the anger out of my voice.

He hesitated on the other end. I barked his name again.

"Victor! You with me?"

More shuffling. "Yeah, sorry Tommy. I'm trying to keep this private but there's guys moving around in here and I don't want anyone to hear me. Jess told me you wanted her to keep a low profile."

I felt my pulse rise. "What do you mean, you talked to her? When...recently?"

I had only said that to her at Michael's house.

"Yeah, last night, late. She called me from a cell phone. I almost didn't pick up because I didn't recognize the number, but I finally did answer and it was her. She was on a borrowed phone. She wanted me to come and see her, to bring her cigs and other stuff."

"And you didn't, right?" It took everything I had to stay calm. I could feel the blood rushing to my face. It hurt. I was sure he could hear the anger in my voice, and I knew the answer before he said it.

"I did, Tommy. She said it would be okay, that nobody knew where she was. I went to her apartment first and picked up some of the things she needed. She gave me good directions and I found the place pretty easily. We hung out a couple of hours and then I left. Nobody saw me."

I couldn't believe the stupidity. "You fucking

moron. How do you know that nobody saw you? Everyone at the Catwalk knows you two are friends. If I was looking for her, I would make sure I knew where you were every off hour, knowing that you would lead me to her. You did just that."

I disconnected and called Michael's house. There was no answer.

Throwing on some clothes, I grabbed my .22 and my sap, then ran out to the parking garage. It hurt to run and took me a minute to get my bearings. I finally remembered the space where I had parked, on the first level. I climbed the stairs quickly. My face was throbbing again, and movement of any kind wasn't coming easily. When I got to the car, I was winded but able to get in, start the car, and head out towards the exit. I paid at the booth and steered the car towards the connector to West Haven.

I drove quickly, weaving in and out of traffic as much as possible, running lights. I was hoping that the cops would see me doing it and I would take them with me to the house. It might have been paranoia, but I could feel it in my gut that something was wrong.

Arriving at the house in record time, I pulled into the back driveway space nearest the back entrance. I went in the lower foyer and ran up the stairs to the second-floor apartment, calling out Jessika's name on the way up. There was no answer. When I got to the door, I saw that it had been forcibly pushed open, with the bolt lock pulled away from the molding. I took out my gun and went in, calling out for Jess. One of the kitchen chairs was on its side. I righted it and moved slowly into the front rooms. The living room was in complete disarray, and I wasn't sure at first if there had been a tussle there or if that's the way it typically looked. Michael wasn't the neatest person around and, from my visits to her apartment, I knew Jessika wasn't exactly Martha Stewart.

I did a quick survey of the bedrooms, then raced down the back stairs, out into the yard and over to the entrance to the studio. The door was open. I went in slowly, calling out to Vince. He wasn't in the front kitchen but as I started down the hallway, I got the strong smell of gasoline. I looked through the glass studio window and saw Vince laying on the floor, writhing. He was coughing and spitting, and his clothes, hair and beard were soaked with gasoline mixed with blood. I grabbed a towel off of the console and knelt by him. He was keeping his eyes closed to keep out the gasoline and screamed when I touched his shoulder.

"It's me, Vince, it's Tommy. Michael's friend. Whoever did this is gone. I'm handing you a towel that you can use to wipe your eyes with."

I was suspect as to how clean it was, but it was all we had at that moment. He took it and tried to get as much of the gasoline off as possible. When he had his eyes open, he started on his hair.

"Vince, Jessika is gone, and her life could be in danger. I'm sure you didn't know the guys who did this but how long ago was it? How long have you been lying here?"

He looked at me with daggers in his eyes and spit out, "One guy. Guido-looking asshole. Busted in and hit me hard a coupla times. I was listening to a playback and didn't hear him at first. The next thing I know he's banging on me. Poured this shit all over me, took out a lighter, and threatened to light me up. I screamed I had no idea, that I sleep out here and don't know what goes on in the house. He screamed some more, asking me which apartment. I had to tell him she was on the second floor. He was gonna torch me!"

I nodded. Not sure anyone would have kept their mouth shut, given the circumstances.

"Vince, how long ago? When did this happen?"

"Not long, twenty minutes maybe? He took off when I told him the floor she was on. I'm guessing he went into the house and grabbed the girl. I heard the car take off, but it was all I could do to try and keep that stuff out of my mouth and eyes. I wasn't sure what I was gonna do. Michael's in New York and no one's due here for a few days. I'm glad you got here!"

Yeah, just not quick enough. Trullo had Jessika and it was anyone's guess what he might do to her. I needed to go.

"Vince, I gotta leave. He's got the girl so he won't come back. He's acting on his own so there's no one else backing him up. You'll be safe. Lock the studio door, though. Yes?"

He nodded that he would, and I went back into the house and up to the second floor. I had scanned the place quickly but took a little more time now. I wanted to see if she had taken her cell phone. Her bag was gone, he had evidently allowed her to take that. I had one shot.

When I was at her apartment earlier, I had uploaded a tracking app on her phone. She didn't know it was there. If she had her phone with her, and he hadn't taken it away from her, I had an outside chance of finding her.

I raced down the back stairs to the rental, got in and

sped out to the main street. I drove down Elm Street and got on the highway to New Haven, getting off at Long Wharf and jockeying my way over to Wooster Street. I doubted Trullo would come back there but it was as central a place to start from as anywhere else. I had tried to find an address for him but came up empty.

I was hoping he lived close to the neighborhood and that the club and the app would lead me to him. And her.

I drove around all the surrounding streets, hoping to hear the blips that would indicate her phone was close, but there was nothing. I couldn't be sure she even had it with her, that he hadn't taken it away from her or disabled it. He could have thrown her bag and its contents away on the side of the road somewhere or in a garbage can. It could be anywhere...and so could they.

After a few hours driving around and getting nothing, I headed back to Wooster Street and Delmonico's social club. It looked dark inside, but I got out and rapped on the door as hard as possible without breaking the glass. There was no answer.

I was running out of possibilities. I got back in the car and ran through different scenarios in my head, but nothing made much sense. I was still groggy, but the pain was making me angrier. I had to do something before it was too late.

I decided to go back to where this whole thing started and drove towards the Catwalk. It was early in the afternoon, but they would be open and would hopefully lead me towards finding her.

TWENTY-TWO

There was a parking space fairly close to the front. After pulling into the space, I got out and walked towards the entrance but stopped short a few cars up the street. There, parked almost in front, was the black Caddy that had been watching me previously—possibly the one that Trullo had been driving when he hit me. It meant either Delmonico, Trullo or both were inside the club. If it was Delmonico, and Trullo went rogue like I thought, he might help me find the girl. If it was just Trullo inside, I was too late.

I paid the cover and went through both sets of doors, waiting just inside until my eyes adjusted to the darkness. I scanned the bar first and saw that Jennifer was on again. She came right over when I sat down on a stool close to the door.

"Hey there. Back again so soon! Red Stripe?"

She already had one out of the cooler, so I nodded yes. She put it down in front of me and I could see her grimace.

"Yikes, what happened to your face?"

I tried to smile.

"What's the cliché, you should see the other guy? Will that fly?"

She smiled back and shook her head. "You must have really pissed someone off."

"It's what I do." I put two twenties on the bar and slid them towards her, keeping my hand on top of them. "For the beer and for some info, yes?"

She continued to smile and nodded almost imperceptibly. She didn't want anyone to see what she was doing, other than schmoozing with a customer. I pressed on.

"Do you know a guy named Trullo and, if you do, is he here now? He's usually part of Anthony Delmonico's crew. Or are they both here?"

She continued to look at me but her eyes darted towards the private alcove. I would have missed it if I wasn't watching closely. I nodded and pushed the money closer. She took one twenty and said, "For the beer," then pushed the other twenty back to me. I put it in my pocket, downed the beer and got off the stool, slowly turning toward the alcove.

I found a small open table that was near the back of the club that gave me a direct view of the alcove Trullo was in. There were two women with him. No one else. The women looked like they were dancers, probably between performances.

Inside the alcove, a leather banquette curved around the inside, with two chairs outside facing in. Anyone sitting on the far right of the booth would have an obstructed view towards the stage. Trullo was on the banquette in the middle, looking out toward the room. His view of the back of the club was blocked by one of the women. The other woman was also on the banquette in the farthest seat on the left, with Trullo leaning towards her, almost bent sideways at the waist. He seemed inebriated.

I needed to do this fast. There were three women working on stage and the music accompanying them was the kind of bombastic heavy metal that could work to my advantage. I got up and sidled towards the alcove, trying to stay out of Trullo's sight line. When I was few feet away from the booth, I placed the sap in the palm of my right hand. One of the women in the booth turned to look at me but before she could say anything or yell, I forced my way into the booth next to Trullo and brought my right up across as hard as I could, aiming for the bridge of his nose. It was right on target. Blood shot across the table and hit the dancer with her back to the club in the face. She and Trullo both started screaming but it was lost in the loud music. My left hand was holding the .22 in my jacket pocket and I jammed it into Trullo's side, barking into his ear for him to get up, keep quiet and move out of the booth. With the sap back in my pocket, I used my free hand to pat him down, finding his car key fob and cell phone but no gun. I was surprised, thinking he would be carrying. I grabbed the keys and phone, then motioned for him to follow me.

To his credit, he didn't fight me and did as I asked. Pain has a way of making one compliant. We slid out of the booth and moved quickly towards the exit. Neither of the bouncers intervened. They barely looked our way as we went out the door.

Once outside, I pushed him towards his car and hit the button on the fob to unlock the doors, opening the back door that was closest to us and pushing him inside. I had made sure to wear gloves. I got in after him and forced him to get as far down onto the floor as possible, behind the driver's seat. I yelled for him to put his hands on the seat as if he was praying. He did as he was told. The blood from his nose was still coming down all over his shirt and he was trying hard to sniff it back in. I had grabbed a set of plastic handcuffs from the apartment and wrapped them around his wrists, pulled the draw tight, and pushed him further down in the area behind the front seat. He made a weird noise, a cross between choking and whimpering. It occurred to me that I had to get what I needed quickly before he passed out.

"Where's the girl? Where's Jessika?"

The rear passenger door was still open, and I didn't want to attract any more attention than necessary. I closed it and asked again, using my left foot on his neck to drive my question home.

He had started to cough and blood went all over the back seat. He was trying to talk through it, but it was so faint, I could barely hear his answer. I raised my voice to a growl.

"Again, where is she?"

I leaned over to see if I could understand him and heard him say, barely more than a whisper, "She's with Anthony."

I sat back, confused, trying to piece this together. He had tried to warn me off the case when he hit me. The what and the how of that warning had led me to think he had gone rogue, that he had his own thing for her and that this was personal. If I was to believe him now, this was all coming back on Delmonico.

"Was this about the stuff Delmonico was missing from when they were together?"

His eyes were closing. I jostled him with my foot again and leaned down closer to him, yelling at the back of his head.

"Was it?!"

He coughed hard again and more blood sprayed onto the floor. After a few seconds, he found his voice and garbled out, "Yes."

Yanking him up while opening the door, I used the key fob to open the trunk. Grabbing his hair with one hand and his wrists with the other, I was able to pull him from the car and push him in, slamming it down hard.

If it hit him in the head, all the better. I got behind the wheel and held it tight, trying to steady my breathing. I wasn't sure what I needed to do next, but I knew time was a serious consideration, that I needed to find her as quickly as possible or it would be too late. I headed towards the social club.

TWENTY-THREE

I pulled a U-turn on East Street and sped down to where Chapel Street began, then over to Wooster Street. I could hear Trullo moaning in the trunk, but I had no idea what I was going to do with him. I decided that I would go with whatever inspiration hit me in the moment, although my track record with that kind of problem solving wasn't always stellar.

I pulled into the same space on Wooster where I had done my original surveillance. The club was still dark. I wasn't sure what to do. I couldn't shake the feeling that the longer it went, the greater the chance that Jessika would be hurt. I considered trying to find Delmonico's apartment but dismissed it quickly. I didn't believe he would have taken her there but, even if he did, he would most likely have a small army guarding the place. The only card I could play was Trullo, who was now kicking the trunk lid of his own car from the inside.

I pulled out and drove down Wooster Street to the end, getting up on the connector to I-95. Halfway over the Q Bridge, I moved into the right lane and got off at the exit for the harbor. I turned left at the end of the exit and drove down a road that ran parallel to the water, until I came to a cluster of industrial buildings, with a new development going in between. A makeshift dirt driveway led towards the back of the development and a new building that was just in the early stages of being framed out. I pulled behind it.

I had called Reilly from the car before I left Wooster Street and he was already waiting there, with the motor of his old Audi running. I pulled next to him so that our driver seat windows were parallel, cop-style. He looked at me and spoke first.

"Yo. Pretty secluded. How do you know about this place?"

There was no time to waste on small talk.

"Saw it a few weeks ago. Are you ready?"

He nodded and I pulled up until the trunks were aligned. He popped his open from inside the car and got out. I was already out of the Caddy and had the .22 in my hand. I used the fob to open the trunk and was met with a barrage of obscenities. I leaned in and put the gun up against his nose and pressed.

"I can hit you again and not stop this time. Keep your mouth shut."

He quieted down and I yanked him up and forced him out of the trunk to a standing position. He was wobbly but I pushed him towards the Audi and forced him into Reilly's trunk. It was much smaller, and I could hear him whimpering. I pushed him in on his stomach, took out his cell from my pocket, then leaned in to his tied hands and pressed his right index finger against the button on his smart phone. It opened up immediately. I slammed the trunk lid.

I looked at the call log. There had been a number of missed calls from "AD", the last being twenty minutes ago. If they didn't hear from him, they would come looking for him. Soon.

Reilly had been leaning against his car with his arms folded.

"So, what am I supposed to do with him now? This is the second time you've involved me in a kidnapping."

I shot him a glance. "And just like the last time, this mutt isn't gonna say anything or go to the cops. It would bring too much heat."

I paused to take a breath, then said, "Follow me back to the Catwalk. I left the rental there and we can leave this car there, where I found it. Then you can take me back to my place so I can see if there's any messages there from Jessika. Maybe Delmonico just put a scare into her and let her go. She might be trying to call me at home."

The words rang hollow as they left my mouth. She would have called my cell. I was grasping at straws. Reilly knew it and stared at me but, to his credit, didn't say a word. He nodded and got in his car.

I spun the Caddy around and took off for the street. Reilly stayed behind me as we got up on the highway, drove back over the bridge and got off at the Hamilton exit. Jockeying around the back streets, we finally hit East Street and I pulled in front of the Catwalk. There was a space open that was close to where the car had been originally, and I pulled into it. I locked it and took the fob with me. Let them work to get the car back.

Reilly pulled his car up just as I finished, and I got

in. We continued down East Street and turned down Grand and in ten minutes we pulled up in front of my apartment.

Trullo had been intermittently kicking in the trunk but had gone silent over the last few minutes. Reilly kept his eyes forward when he spoke.

"What now?"

I looked at him and a new wave of exhaustion came over me. I was afraid of what the eventual outcome of this situation would be. The person who hired me was missing, I had a mobster in the trunk of my friend's car, and I had no idea what to do next. All the clichés applied. I was out of my depth and over my head. And I didn't know what to tell Reilly.

"Stay here. I'm going to run in and see if she left a message. If she didn't, we go over to Delmonico's club again and see if they're back there. If they're not, I'm outa options."

He still hadn't looked at me. I knew he believed we were too late but didn't want to say it yet.

"How about the cops? Maybe we should go down there and report this?"

I shook my head. "Not yet. I'm hoping she's fine. We have no proof about any of this and we have a guy in the trunk of your car. Would you believe us if we told you this story?"

He continued to stare out the window. After a few seconds, he shook his head.

I got out of his car and started towards the door of my apartment building. As I was passing a car that was sitting two spaces up from where we had parked, two men got out and flashed badges at me. Plainclothes detectives. I recognized one from an earlier case, one where a young student that I had gotten to know had been beaten so badly he was in a coma. When I went to see him, there were cops there, grilling me for information on the case I was working. He was one of them. Mendillo or Melillo, something like that. He spoke first.

"Tommy Shore? Can we speak to you about Jessika Quinlan?"

I looked at him closely. He gave nothing away in his face or eyes, no sense of recognition. I nodded and asked if they wanted to come inside to do it, trying not to look back at Reilly's car.

"No, we'd like you to come down to the station, if you don't mind." He said it quietly, but I knew it wouldn't make much difference if I minded or not. I shrugged okay and the other cop opened the back door of the unmarked car. I got in, catching a side glimpse of Reilly pulling away. The two cops didn't say a word as we headed down to the main police station, keeping their eyes straight ahead.

Serious as a heart attack.

TWENTY-FOUR

They pulled up to a space in front of the police department building. I had only been here a few times before, mostly to ask questions of the few cops I knew. The reason I thought I might be here now filled me with dread.

Once inside the station, they led me to a small room, deep in the bowels of the building. The cop I didn't know told me to have a seat, pointing at a single chair facing the door, then left. The room was exactly what I pictured an interrogation room to be like...ugly and barren and non-descript. I sat down on the uncomfortable wooden chair and waited. There were two other chairs facing mine on the other side of a table in the middle of the room. I looked around and saw the camera up near the ceiling in the far corner. Nothing else.

I took out my phone to see if there was a message from Jessika, but I couldn't get any cell service. I was still holding out hope that Delmonico didn't do anything to her, maybe just roughed her up a bit, but that hope was fading quickly.

After ten minutes or so, the door opened and the two cops who picked me up came in. The one I sort of knew sat across from me at the table, while the other one leaned on the wall near the door. He had his arms folded and there was nothing on his face I could read. I looked at Melillo/Mendillo and shrugged. He had a folder with him that he carefully placed on the table between us. I could see the tab had Jessika's name printed on it in pen. He spoke first.

"I'm Detective Melillo and this is Detective Egan. You and I met briefly at the emergency room when James Bitten had been assaulted and you had been hired to watch his girlfriend. Do you remember me?"

I nodded and didn't say anything. Let him talk.

"Good. What can you tell us about Jessika Quinlan?"

I looked at him for a good twenty seconds. I wasn't under arrest. No rights had been read to me and they had brought me here civilly, no cuffs or threats. I had been searched for a weapon, but they had let me keep all my personal stuff. It was clear to me that this would be a good time to bring them into the equation.

I told them almost everything. About meeting her in the bar after she sought me out, the threats she had received, both the doll and the dead cat. Going to the Catwalk and looking at the tapes. Watching Delmonico's club until I was made and invited in. Getting waylaid and then assaulted by Trullo. The incessant phone calls she received and eventually hiding her in West Haven. Her seeing her friend Victor and then being taken from the house in West Haven. I left out the part about grabbing Trullo.

Melillo just looked at me. Egan hadn't moved at all from where he stood, just kept shaking his head. Melillo finally spoke.

"And neither of you thought to call the police? Thought you'd play gumshoe, find the bad guy, solve the mystery and ride off into the sunset on a white horse, right?"

I waited for more. After a minute or so, when I realized he was waiting for me, I asked him the question. It came out softly. My throat had begun to close up.

"Did you find her?"

He stared at me again and then pushed the folder towards me, flipping it open. There was a stack of four or five photographs of a dead body. A woman. Jessika.

I closed my eyes for a few seconds, trying to steady myself and gather my thoughts. It pissed Melillo off and he grabbed the photographs and spread them out on the table, yelling, "Open your fucking eyes and look at them! Look what this little game of pretend has done. Look at her!"

I looked at the photos. I could see she had suffered. There was a lot of blood caking her hair and she had bruises over her body and face. I felt my anger building but knew I needed to control my reactions until I got out of here. I looked up at Melillo and slowly spoke.

"Where did you find her?"

He shook his head, sighed, and began shuffling the photos back into the folder. "That's what you want to know?"

The other cop spoke up.

"We found her a couple of hours ago in one of the

dumpsters that the McDonald's on Kimberly Avenue uses in West Haven, along with her handbag. Somebody did a number on her, worked her over bad. Her neck had been snapped, her skull bashed in. She suffered."

I could tell he was watching me for a reaction. He continued talking.

"Your card was in her bag, along with some other things. How we knew to contact you. No wallet, no cash, no cell phone. We knew this wasn't a robbery, that this was something else. Your story puts another spin on it."

I nodded then looked back to Melillo.

"Am I under arrest? Am I a suspect? Can I leave or do I need a lawyer?"

Melillo scoffed and said, "You can go. But I would keep a low profile if I were you. You're in way over your head. These are bad guys you're fucking with. They may not be what they used to be here but that don't mean they're not out there doing bad things. You'll end up just like her if you're not careful."

He paused, watching for my reaction. I tried to keep everything that was going on inside my head off my face. I could tell he was done with talking to me.

"Get out of here. If you hear or see anything that could help with this, call me. We will have more questions for you later so be available." He slid his card toward me, and I took it without looking at it and slipped into my jacket pocket.

Egan opened the door and pointed down the hallway that they brought me in from. I got up, left and found my way outside. I called Reilly as soon as I hit the steps down to the street. He answered immediately.

"Tommy, where are you? I have the guy here, down in the catacombs, the basement apartments of the Taft. He still has your cuffs on him. I wasn't sure what to do so I brought him here. Nobody saw us come into the building or come down here."

I told him what had transpired with the cops as I ran towards my building, telling him I would be there in about ten minutes. I didn't tell him Jessika was dead. I wanted to work Trullo on my own.

TWENTY-FIVE

The Taft Building was once one of the premiere hotels in New Haven. After a new, fancier hotel had been built, it was clear the city couldn't sustain two. It had been shuttered in the seventies until 1981, when it was reopened and converted to apartments. Where I currently resided.

During Prohibition, the owners had built a speakeasy in the basement. It thrived for years until the laws changed. Afterwards, the owners tried to convert the basement space to apartments, but they were drafty and noisy and after a few years were left dormant. But you could still access them if you knew how.

I went in the front doors and got on the elevator, going up one floor. When it stopped, I pushed the button marked "B" and it took me back down, past the lobby floor and to the basement. Once there, I found the exit door that led to the sub-basement, the once thriving speakeasy. There were still a number of rooms down there that had furniture and mattresses, but no one ever came down there, unless they needed to hide something.

It was dark so I used the flashlight app on my phone to light the way. As I made my way down the corridor towards the back rooms, I could hear feet shuffling, along with muffled choking sounds coming from one of the last rooms on the left.

Walking into the room, I could see Reilly sitting on a chair in the corner. Trullo was laying on his stomach on a dirty mattress that had been used recently in one of my cases involving two people on the run, trying not to be found. This part of the hotel had become a sanctuary for them. The pair had jerry-rigged an extension cord to the electrical system and had left a small lamp behind when they'd gone. Reilly had turned it on, and it cast off a weak light that gave the room an eerie atmosphere.

Reilly used his chin to point towards Trullo. "He's been mouthing off, so I stuck an old towel down his throat. I found it down here so it mighta been a tad dusty. I left the cuffs on."

I walked over and grabbed Trullo by the shoulder and flipped him on his back. His face was red and he was having trouble breathing through his busted nose. There was dried blood caked on both sides of his face. It made him look clownish. I leaned over and pulled the old piece of towel out of his mouth. He gasped for breath and started coughing vehemently. I waited until it stopped and then spoke to him in a calm monotone.

"Bobby, I'm going to ask you some questions. Your answers will dictate how I proceed. If I think you're lying to me, I will hurt you. Badly. Understood?"

He coughed some more but nodded yes.

"Tell me what happened after you grabbed Jessika

at the house in West Haven. Everything, up until the minute I grabbed you at the club. Leave nothing out."

He looked at me with hate in his eyes and said, "Go fuck yourself. You have no idea who you're messing with. Tony's gonna have your head on a plate."

I walked over and grabbed a wooden chair that was in the far corner of the room, pulling it over to the mattress where Trullo was laying. I nodded towards Reilly to help me, and we each grabbed an arm, pulled him upright, and then violently sat him back down in the chair.

I took the .22 out of my pocket and held it with the chamber in the palm of my hand. Standing in front of him, I told Trullo that, if he didn't answer every question quickly and completely, I would bring the gun down across his nose as hard as I could. I continued to keep my voice in a low, even monotone, to make him understand I was serious. Surprisingly, it did the trick. He looked at me, sighed and I could see most of the fight go out of him. I had been betting that he couldn't take any more pain and I was right. He nodded his cooperation.

"Tell me what happened. Like I said, don't leave anything out."

He ran through the whole story. About following Victor after she called him to come visit her at the studio in West Haven. About getting into the studio and making Vincent tell him where she was by first beating on him, then pouring gasoline over him and threatening to light him on fire. About breaking into the house, grabbing Jess and dragging her by the hair out to his car. About taking her to Delmonico and leaving her with him. About hearing her scream as he left

Delmonico and how he headed to the Catwalk to get drunk.

I watched him as he struggled to talk through the broken nose and the crap left in his mouth and throat from the rag Reilly had stuck in there. It took everything I had not to beat on him myself when he was done telling me the chain of events.

"You're telling me that you didn't know she's dead, right, that Delmonico killed her? That he beat her senseless and then broke her neck?"

I could hear Reilly moving behind me as I asked Trullo this and felt him rush past me and hit Trullo on the side of the head with a small metal box that must have been left down here by the previous occupants. Trullo fell sideways off the chair and back onto the mattress. His head started bleeding immediately. I pushed Reilly back and away from him. I had forgotten that I hadn't told him what the cops had shown me. This was news to him, and he reacted accordingly, but I still had information that I needed to get.

I knelt down onto the mattress and showed him the .22 again.

"Tell me what Delmonico wanted from her or I'll keep hitting you until you can no longer breathe. I will kill you and dump you in a garbage bin, like she had been. What did she take? I'm not buying the ring and watch bullshit. There's more to it than that. What was it?"

He shook his head and started to whimper. "I can't. He'll kill me."

I pressed the gun down hard onto the bridge of his nose and he screamed. When I thought the pain had subsided, I placed it there again.

"I can do this all night. This place is soundproof, and no one knows you're here. Tell me what I need to know."

The blood from where Reilly hit him was running down his face and into his mouth. Breathing out of his nose was impossible and he started to choke. I rolled him over onto his stomach and pressed the gun at the back of his neck.

"I've changed my mind. I'm running out of patience, asshole, and I'm ready to put you out of your misery. Tell me what she took."

I could hear a muffled response, so I stood up and grabbed a pillow. Using my foot to flip him on his back, I leaned over closer to him and held the gun behind the pillow and yelled for him to tell me. He finally had enough and yelled that he'd tell me. Spitting out blood, he said, "A book. She took Delmonico's book."

I scowled. "What book?"

He spit out some more blood until he could talk, then looked up and said, "Delmonico kept a log book of every transaction that he's ever been involved in. It's got the names of other made guys and their numbers. Lots of names. It also has their rackets and the amounts of money they bring in. It was his safety net."

I pulled my foot away and stood there, thinking that a book like that would have information in it that neither Delmonico or any of the guys in the book would ever want to get out. But it didn't make sense that Jessika would have grabbed it unless she knew what it was and wanted to use it somehow.

Trullo struggled to get the rest out.

"Jessika knew what Tony wanted but she refused to give it back. Then she got you involved. Made it even harder. Tony got pissed when you hid her away and told me to find her and bring her to him. I did as I was told. But she didn't have it. I searched her place. I'm surprised he killed her without finding out what she did with it."

I looked over at Reilly. He was looking at the floor and shaking his head. I walked over and whispered to him, "I need to go to her apartment and see if I can find it. In the meantime, I'm not sure what to do with him. Whattya think?"

He looked up and laughed.

"Now you're asking me for my opinion? I wanted out of this thing from the jump."

I couldn't tell if he was angry, tired or both. I decided right there I needed to remove him from any further involvement.

"Never mind. I'm gonna call Mickey and get his advice on what to do next. I'm way over my head here."

Reilly recoiled at the mention of Mickey's name. I knew Mickey made him nervous, but we were boxed in. He thought for a few seconds and finally said, "Do what ya gotta do."

Looking back at Trullo, I could see he had started crying but felt no empathy. He may not have done it himself, but he was certainly a catalyst for Jess's death. I needed to find a method to take him out of the picture without letting Delmonico know I had him.

"Stay here and watch him? I'm going up to my apartment to change clothes and make some calls. I'll know what to do when I come back down. Maybe a half hour?"

He nodded and I offered him the gun. He shook his head. "I won't need it. He won't be any more trouble."

I took the elevator upstairs and got off on my floor. The weight of what happened was starting to register and I could feel the energy being drained out of my body. I had let Jessika down and gotten her killed and it started to sweep over me. It was only a matter of time before it would turn into uncontrollable anger.

TWENTY-SIX

I went to my apartment, changed into some fresh clothes, grabbed my lock-picking kit, then I called Mickey. He answered on the first ring.

"Tommy. Call you right back." I hung up quickly. The matter-of-fact tone in his voice made me wonder if he already knew. He called me back a minute later on a burner.

There was a slight hesitation and then he said, "Okay, this is a safe line. What's up?"

"Mick, I've got some trouble."

"Yeah, I heard. Word on the street is you snatched one of Delmonico's guys. That true?"

I told him it was, then laid out the rest of it. How I'd hidden Jessika away because I thought Trullo was after her from some sick obsession he had for her. How he had found out where she was and brought her to Delmonico. I went through to where I grabbed him at the strip club and then the cops picking me up afterwards to grill me. I told him almost everything, including Trullo telling me that it was Delmonico who actually wanted her and about the book with the names and numbers and addresses of other mob guys.

There was no sound for a minute or so. I thought we had been disconnected.

"Mickey, you there?"

He cleared his throat and asked, "Where's Trullo now?"

I took a deep breath. "I've got him, hidden away, cuffed, with someone watching him. I don't know what my next move should be. I'm really over my head on this."

He scoffed. "Ya think? You snatched a soldier that's affiliated with a prominent guy, a made guy. When Delmonico puts it together, he's not gonna just let it go."

I waited for him to say more. When nothing came, I said, "Mick, I need your help here. I'm gonna try and find the book but I can't be worrying about Trullo while I do it. Once I find it, I can maybe use it to ensure my safety."

Mickey scoffed again. "Listen, Tommy, this mutt will not back off you, book or no book. And what I do know about him is that nobody's off limits. Not family, not friends. He don't care. Hang on."

I waited. After a few minutes, I heard movement in the background until Mickey came back on the phone. "Listen, I'm gonna send a coupla guys to meet you and take Trullo off your hands. Remember that diner in Hamden where we met once? There. They'll be parked in the back lot, black Escalade. Leave him cuffed and gagged. We'll take it from there. Be about an hour. Call me after it's done."

I thought for a few seconds, then agreed. This was getting out of hand, but I had to do something. At the very least, it would allow me time to go to Jessika's place and see if I could find the book or figure out where it could be. I said I would see his guys in an hour and hung up.

I took the elevator back down to the basement apartments. It was pretty much as when I'd left except Trullo had pissed himself and the odor enveloped the entire room. I looked at Reilly, but he just shook his head.

"I wasn't gonna bring him to the john so he pissed his pants. Not such a tough guy anymore, eh?"

He said it to me but loud enough so Trullo knew it was intended for him. I pulled Reilly out into the hall, and using a whisper said, "I spoke to my friend. He's gonna send a couple of his guys and I'm going to give them Trullo. They'll take care of watching this asshole. After that, I'll go to Jess's apartment and see if I can find the book. I have no idea what to do with it if I find it but maybe I can use it to negotiate with Delmonico. It could come in handy somewhere down the line."

Reilly looked at me with skepticism and said, "They're gonna watch this guy? Yeah, right."

I shrugged. I didn't care what happened to him. I went back into the room and over to Trullo, yanking him up on his feet. I took the cloth we used before and shoved it back in his mouth. He made noises until I took out the .22.

"Keep quiet and nothing happens. Make any kind of noise, try anything and one goes in each of your kneecaps. Understood?"

He settled down and nodded. The smell coming off him was making me nauseous, so I bent down and grabbed one of the dirty sheets off the mattress, wrapping it around his waist. It dampened the aroma a bit and would hopefully keep the piss off the floor of the Audi's trunk.

I turned to Reilly.

"Last thing I need from you is to take me to go get the rental. I left it parked down in front of the Catwalk. I can transfer him into that trunk and take him to where we're meeting. Where'd you park? Get the car and pull into the alley off Temple. Back in if you can."

He nodded, told me that he was in the garage and left to go get the car. I waited ten minutes then dragged Trullo out through the back exit and out onto the street, pulling him down towards the alley where Reilly was. Holding on to the sheet around his waist, I spun him around when we got close to the car and pushed him back into the trunk, slammed the lid down, then got in the car. Reilly pulled out slowly and drove me to the Catwalk.

I pointed out the rental to Reilly. Using the fob as soon as we were close enough, I popped open the rental's trunk. Reilly pulled the Audi up as close as possible, aligning the trunks side by side. I jumped out as he released his trunk and pulled Trullo out and back into the rental trunk. I closed the Audi trunk, then banged on it, signaling Reilly he was clear to go. He tore out and I watched as he went up the street and turned left to go back to his apartment.

I got into the rental and headed towards Hamden, reminding myself to breathe.

TWENTY-SEVEN

It was already getting dark. I took the back streets through the city and into Hamden. The diner was located on Dixwell Avenue in a tough section of town. It was a good choice. If anybody saw the exchange happening, they would look away and keep their mouths shut.

I pulled in and saw the Escalade parked in the back of the lot, tucked away in a corner. There was an open space next to it. I thought it was fortunate until I realized that the two guys in the Caddy were keeping people from parking there. One of them was standing outside on the passenger side, his huge arms folded across his chest. As I got closer, I could see he had a toothpick between his teeth and was rolling it around in his mouth, waiting. Probably saw it in a movie and thought it made him look good.

I pulled into the empty space, popped open the trunk using the inside button and was halfway out of the car when I heard the big guy order me to stay inside the car. He grabbed Trullo and pulled him out of the trunk, catching a whiff of his stench.

"Jesus Christ, this guy stinks, smells like he pissed himself. We're keeping him wrapped in this sheet for the drive back."

I watched in the rearview mirror as he manhandled Trullo like a puppet, pushed him to the back of the Cadillac, opened the hatch, jockeyed him in, closed the hatch and got back in the car. The two goons pulled out and drove off. All in under a minute.

Waiting a few minutes before pulling out, I got on the Merritt Parkway towards New Haven, taking the first exit after the tunnel and following Whalley Avenue into Westville and over to Jess's apartment complex.

I parked as far as I could from the entrance, unsure if Delmonico might already have someone watching the place. I looked around but nothing appeared out of the ordinary. Getting out, I stayed close to the other parked cars and away from areas where the lot lights illuminated things. I got to the door quickly and pressed all of the buttons. Someone answered and I said, "Pizza delivery." The buzzer sounded and I went in and up to the second floor.

I could see the yellow tape from down the hallway and knew the police had already been here. Taking out my lock kit as I moved down the hallway, I pulled out the basic tools. I had taken an online course on how to do this and had practiced on a variety of locks at home. Most of these apartments used cheap locks and it only took a few seconds until I was in, ducking underneath the crime tape so as not to disturb it. I closed the door quickly, as quietly as possible.

The front room was in shambles. Someone had tossed it haphazardly and without concern. The pillows from the couch had been ripped open and there were feathers everywhere. Books and magazines had been thrown about, cleared from the shelves. The cushions from the easy chair were on the floor, with long slits down the sides and stuffing poking out.

The kitchen was an even bigger mess. All of the cabinets had been opened and food boxes had been taken down from shelves and gone through, left on the counter or poured into the sink. A container that once held sugar had been emptied and much of it had spilled onto the floor. Whoever had gone through the place had been thorough. The few things that had been in her freezer had been taken out and now laid on the floor, thawing out. The meat was starting to turn gray, and it wouldn't be long before it began to smell. In a few days, the stench would be unbearable.

Before moving to the bedroom, I made a quick look around her bathroom. It was much the same, with toiletries and towels everywhere and all the drawers pulled out and emptied.

A quick glance around her bedroom told me that whoever did this spent a lot of time in this room. Clothes had been taken from the closet and bureau and tossed everywhere. The top mattress to her bed had been pushed off and almost onto the floor. The box spring beneath it had long knife slits down the center and the sides. It was almost impossible to move about the room easily. I made a quick search and went back out to the living room.

I pushed my anger and sadness aside and tried to clear my head. Delmonico had clearly sent someone over here to search the place, but they must have found nothing. The cops probably came later, surveyed the place, made it a crime scene and left. They would have done a cursory search as well.

I tried to put myself in Jess's head, to see what her frame of mind might have been. She was savvy enough to not keep the book here or in her car. Where else would she hide it? There was little privacy at the Catwalk so that would certainly be out. I didn't get the feeling she would have risked giving it to Victor or any of the other dancers to hold for her. So what did that leave?

I had already been in the apartment too long and knew I had to leave. I glanced around the place one last time, moving again from the front room to the kitchen when I spotted a small hook with one key on it, just to the left of the switch for the garbage disposal, near the sink. Thinking it might be to a lock box or a cabinet, I scanned the front rooms again but saw nothing that looked like it might fit into it. I went back into the bedroom and the bathroom, but it was much the same. I left, taking the key with me, hoping an idea might come to me. My luck with that had not been very good lately.

Back in the car, I stared at the key. There was something about it that seemed familiar to me but I couldn't bring up what it was. I took a deep breath. I realized that I had been going full out for a while now and that I was tired. The full force of what happened to Jess was starting to hit me, and I fought back the depression I knew could take over and cripple me if I let it.

I pulled out of the lot and headed for home.

TWENTY-EIGHT

Once inside my apartment, an overwhelming feeling of failure started to come over me. Trying to fight it, I took an extremely hot shower. That usually helped but didn't work this time. I was exhausted but too wound up to sleep. As I looked around the apartment, it occurred to me that I hadn't had a drink in a while. Perhaps that would help with my clarity. At the very least, it would dampen the feelings I was trying to push aside. I got dressed and went across the street to the Owl.

It wasn't overly crowded but the bar was full, so I sat at one of the easy chairs in the middle of the place. I ordered a Jameson and an Americano from the waitress. She came back with them quickly. I downed the whiskey in two gulps, with the intention of finding that immediate warmth, which I would sustain by the heat of the coffee.

I took the key out of my pocket and studied it. I couldn't shake the notion that it looked familiar to me, that I had seen one like it before. It was small and fairly non-descript, but there were three numbers on it, 124, that were etched into the top part. That was it. I stared at it but nothing resonated. I doubted that Jess could afford a safety deposit box at a bank. I dismissed the thought that it could have been to a pad lock that she used at a health club, doubting that she would keep something with that much value in a locker at the gym.

I sat back in the chair and sipped my coffee. When I looked up, it hit me.

Across a thirty-foot expanse of one side of the Owl was a bank of cigar lockers. The owner had originally sold all of them out when the place had first opened years ago. They cost $300 each and the same amount was required each year to keep them up. Ownership included a cigar on your birthday, which the cigar manager would place in your locker using a duplicate key. The hardcore regulars bought them and kept their stock of cigars in there. I had one when I was flush but gave it up a while ago.

Over the years, the cache of having a locker began to diminish. They weren't humidified and it cost extra money to constantly re-supply them with humidified packs, which the Owl conveniently sold up at the front desk. A lot of guys let them go after the first year. As time went by, the cost of having one came down dramatically and you could now have one for fifty dollars. I remembered that I had first met Jess in the Owl. She may have been coming here before then and maybe heard from the bartenders about the lockers. It would be a perfect space. Hidden in plain sight.

I stood up and went to the first locker. They were numbered, starting at 100 and going up. I followed them across and down, to locker 124. The key went in smoothly and turned easily, opening the locker. There, beneath a sheaf of paperwork, was the book.

I took it out and looked at it. It surprised me. A leather flexi-bound deal, it was about an inch and a half thick, a faded red in color, almost pink. With a snap. Almost feminine. Not at all what I was expecting.

I closed the locker door, turning the key to lock it up again. I decided that I didn't want to chance anyone seeing me looking at it here in the bar, so I slipped it in my waistband and pulled my shirt out to cover it, then went to the front counter, paid my check and went back over to my apartment.

Once inside, I undid the snap and opened the book, recoiling slightly at first glance from what I saw there. On the first three pages, divided into columns and in the tiniest of print, were the names, addresses, and phone numbers of every key player in local New Haven politics. Most I recognized but a few that I didn't. After each name was a series of numbers without notation. Might be dollars but could be anything. No figure was less than four numbers.

After those first few pages, in much the same layout, were the names of prominent businesspeople that I again recognized from briefly scanning the *New Haven Register* every morning. Same deal – numbers followed each name, and each figure was no less than four numbers. Very few began with the number 1. Most started above 5.

After that, there were names I didn't recognize, a list that went on for another ten pages. The difference on these pages was that every name had a series of letter abbreviations after them – HR, SB, BB, FB, and so on. I thought back to what Trullo has said, that the book included each guy's "racket." If that was the case, these could stand for "Horse Racing" or "Baseball" or "Football" and the amounts being bet on them. And if I was right, this book held incriminating information that totaled in the millions. No wonder Delmonico wanted it back so badly.

What wasn't making sense was why Jessika had held out and didn't just give it back to him from the beginning. I didn't get the sense she would have had the ability to withstand even a little pain and I was sure Delmonico would have hurt her to get it back. I was also sure she wouldn't have been able to make any sense of the jottings or even know how find a buyer for the book, even if she wanted to use it to make a quick score.

Unless she had help. Someone who might be able to connect her to the kinds of guys who would find this information valuable. Someone who had access to them, even if it was minimal. Someone like Victor.

I thought back to our first meeting. He had been nervous at the club, kept looking around, and worried that someone might see us talking. Someone who might think that he was telling tales out of school. Someone who might then label him a rat.

He had told me he just worked there and that he wasn't involved with the goings on of the place, and that he was working his way through school. I'm sure they both owed a lot of money for school loans. Maybe Victor saw this as a way to pay off that debt quickly, both his and hers. All it involved was an opportunity. And then Jessika provided that. I needed to find him.

I called the Catwalk. It rang for a long time until a woman finally picked up.

"Catwalk."

I wasn't expecting a woman's voice. I took a friendly but serious tone.

"Hi, I'm looking for Victor, the bartender. Is he there? This is his uncle. There's been a situation in the family."

There was a hesitation. "Uh, hold on." I could hear her talking to someone while she held her hand over the phone. She came back quickly.

"Uh, Victor no longer works here."

I wasn't surprised. Given what had gone on, my guess was he quit right after the cops came looking for him about Jessika. Not a safe bet to let his employers think he might be talking out of school. Especially these employers.

"Any idea where he might have gone, did he leave a forwarding address?"

I heard an abrupt, "No!" and my cell went dead.

I looked in the directory of my cell phone. I remembered asking him to put his number in. I looked under V but it wasn't there. Then I remembered his last name.

"Trang." I said it out loud, then shook my head. Talking to myself. Not a good sign.

The number was in there under his last name and I called it, getting his mailbox. I was going to hang up but decided to leave a message he might respond to.

"Victor, it's Tommy Shore. I'm sure by now you've heard about Jessika. I need to talk to you. I know about everything. I can maybe protect you, but you need to call me. Now."

I hung up, grabbed the book and my gun, and then went out, intent on heading towards Wooster Street and Delmonico's social club.

TWENTY-NINE

I had parked the rental on one of the higher levels in the garage. The staircase leading up to it was locked for some reason, and it took me a little longer to walk all the way around to the other entrance. As I started to go in, my cell rang. It was Victor. I went back outside to take the call and to make sure that I had reception.

"Speak."

The abruptness must have thrown him. "Uh, Tommy, is that you?"

"It is, Victor. You got my message. We need to talk. Right now. Where are you?"

"I went underground. I quit my job at Catwalk. I'm scared out of my mind, screening calls, looking over my shoulder everywhere I go. After what they did to Jess, who knows what they'll do to me. They know we were close."

I took a deep breath. I didn't want to scare him further by getting angry and saying something that would send him running.

"Victor, listen to me. I can protect you, but I need to

meet with you and talk about next steps. I have a lot of questions, the answers to which will help me decide what road to take to put this thing to bed. I can come to you. Where can we meet?"

I could sense him considering this. After a few seconds, he said, "I live in Hamden. There's a ballfield a short drive from me and across the street from the park is a dog walk with a lot. Meet me there. I'll text you the address so you can GPS it."

We hung up and I went up the stairs to the third level and walked the length of it to my rental car. Victor's text came through just as I closed the door. I pulled out of the garage and slowed at the entrance to see if I could spot a possible tail. I didn't see anyone waiting in a car so I proceeded out to the street and down to the highway entrance.

Getting off at the Hamden exit, I doubled back towards the location Victor had texted me. The GPS woman led me down some back streets and I was there in 15 minutes. The ballpark was lit up, but the only people there were a couple of kids playing basketball. Across the street was the dog walk. I couldn't see anyone in there but most of the light was coming from across the street. I pulled in the parking area and waited.

About two minutes in, I saw a figure getting out of a car parked in the shadows near the fence opening for the dog walk. He was wearing a watch cap pulled way down and had his collar up but I could see it was Victor. I swung the car as close as possible and he got in. I pulled a U-turn out of the lot and got back on the streets, driving back through some of the residential neighborhoods.

As a kid, I had lived near this area, and it came back to me quickly. I went down a through street and turned right onto State Street, pulling into the lot of the No Worries brewery and down towards the back, away from the street. I slammed the car into park, reached into my pocket to take out the .22, and turned towards Victor.

"I want the whole story, every detail, leave nothing out. Now!"

I leaned the gun on the top of the seat, near the headrest. Victor's eyes went wide as he looked at it and then looked back at me. He started crying, struggling to catch his breath.

"Tommy, I didn't think he would take it this far. I thought he would pay us and that would be it. We could pay off our debts and get away from here. I never thought he would hurt her. I swear!"

I looked at him, confused.

"Start from the beginning."

He took a deep breath and sat back.

"Jessika and I were more than friends. Much more. We truly loved each other. I met her when I started bartending at the Catwalk and we started going out soon after. We had a lot in common. Both of us were just working there until we had enough money to pay off our loans and get out. We could go to California and start over.

"After a while, I realized that it would take forever to get enough cash to get us out of there. We tried to figure out other things to do to make some quick cash but there was nothing we could do that would give us enough to pay off both our loans and leave us enough for a new life out West."

He paused to catch his breath, glanced again at the gun, then continued.

"I was doing inventory one morning when the owner came in with his goons. They all sat at one of the tables in the club they reserved for the big shots. It looked to me like some kind of business meeting, ya know, except that they were all drinking. Heavy shit, Courvoisier and Brandy, that kind of stuff. They asked me to make drinks. Tony Aprillo took me aside and told me to bring them whatever they wanted and then disappear. I did what I was told.

But when I brought the second round out, I saw that Delmonico was writing stuff in this weird little book. I glanced at it quickly and saw he was about halfway through and that it was already full of thousands of jottings, numbers, names and more. They were talking about betting, games, that kind of stuff. I figured the book was a ledger, a diary of who bet what and who owes."

I looked at Victor and couldn't keep the disdain off my face. It was easy to figure out where this story was going.

"Go on."

He took another deep breath then looked down and closed his eyes, bringing his hand up to his face and using his fingers to rub his temples.

"I knew that Delmonico had a thing for Jess. He had asked her out before, but she refused. I didn't care, he had money and could take her to nice places and give her stuff that I couldn't. She didn't want to at first but I trusted her and she finally said yes. They went out for a while but then he broke it off. We figured that was that. He stayed away from the club. But when he started coming back again on a regular basis, I was betting that he still had a thing for her. That's when the plan began to come to me. Jess and I discussed it. If she could find a way to get back with him, she might be able to get her hands on the book. We could then figure out a way to get him to pay us a bunch of money to get it back. If we did it right, by the time he figured everything out, we'd be on our way west."

I had looked away from him, staring out the front windshield, trying to contain my anger that was building quickly. Victor was getting more upset as he told me the story. Hearing it out loud brought home the lameness of the plan to him.

"You pimped her out?

He shook his head. "We were doing what we had to do."

It took everything I had not to hit him.

"And the doll and the cat?"

He lowered his head further.

"That was me. I did that. We thought we needed a cover story to get you on board. It had to be something gruesome enough that would hold up. We figured it would be enough to convince you to help her.

"Tommy, we really thought it would work. I know he's supposed to be connected and all but I watched the guy a lot. So did Jess. He seemed all talk. Neither of us had any idea he would react this way, that it would get violent."

I looked at him. I no longer cared about keeping the anger out of my voice.

"What did you need me for? Why get me involved?"

He looked down at his hands again and spoke softly.

"I had a friend who knew you, this bartender from Diesel. She told me about the help you gave her girl-friend. I figured we needed Delmonico's attention focused elsewhere. I told Jess exactly what to say and how to act, to get you to take the case. We figured that if there was someone in the club asking questions and looking into everything that was going on, he would keep a low profile. We didn't expect him to sic his attack dog on us. I remember Trullo from the club. He's a psychopath. When you hid Jess away in West Haven, I thought she'd be safe."

I'd had enough. I started yelling.

"And she would have been safe, if you two assholes did what I told you to do. If you had stayed away from her, she'd be alive now. You made it easy. Led them right to her and got her killed!"

I stopped before I got carried away. He had begun sobbing again. I continued.

"I should really walk away from this and let you fend for yourself. Wash my hands of the whole shitty deal and find a way to get the book back to him. But I don't think he'll let it go that easy. You took something from him. He can't let that happen and keep face amongst his cronies. The word will get out that he's soft. He can't afford that, not with what that book means. It's probably worth a couple hundred thousand dollars by itself, maybe more. Not to mention what it could do in the hands of the cops or the FBI."

Victor looked at me with his mouth open.

"You found the book?"

I looked away again. Talking to this kid was useless. He had one thing in his mind. I nodded.

"I did. It wasn't that hard. I have it hidden away."

He was looking out the window. I got the feeling he was trying to think up an angle.

"Do you think maybe we should go to the cops first?"

I was done with him. I backed out of the lot and drove him back to his car. Neither of us said a word until we got to his car.

"Get out."

He had stopped crying and was trying to collect himself.

"Tommy, I need you to know this. I loved her, I truly loved her. She was my everything. All we wanted was a way to go somewhere else and start a new life. I don't know what I'm going to do now without her!"

I looked at him. I could see that there might be pain there but I wasn't sure I believed all of it.

"Victor, the two of you lied to me. The entire time. This whole thing was one big con. When I was at her apartment, Jess seemed scared to death, but I see now it was just acting, part of the ruse. And I bought into it like a first-class dupe. I'm not sure I believe you now."

I repeated my order.

"Get out. Go home. Once you're there, pack some things and try to find a safe place, a place no one knows about. A relative, a friend. Anyplace. Go there. Don't go to the cops. You've got no evidence and it'll only buy you more pain or worse. It'll make you a target."

He persisted. "What are you going to do?"

I looked hard at him.

"You two have put me and the people around me in

harm's way. I've got to go try and fix this mess, so they don't come after us. I will try and include you in the deal. I'm not sure if I can do it but I'm gonna try. My advice to you is to keep as low a profile as possible. I'll reach out and let you know how I make out."

I used the gun to wave him out. He got out and stood by the side of the car as I backed up and pulled away.

Back to Plan A.

THIRTY

I headed back down to State Street, then followed it all the way to Court Street and down Olive Street to Wooster. Once again, the space in front of the new pizza joint was open and I pulled in there.

I waited a while, watching Delmonico's social club. It looked dark inside, but I thought I saw some movement through the window. No one was sitting outside on the chair where I first saw Trullo.

Locking the book in the glove box, I took out my phone and texted a message to Reilly, telling him that, if he didn't hear from me within the hour, he was to call the cops and send them over here. I gave him the make and license plate number of the car and where the book was. I read it over, then sent it.

I checked the .22 to make sure it was fully loaded, put some extra ammo in my jacket pocket, got out of the car and crossed the street to the club.

The door was unlocked when I tried the handle. It surprised me. Maybe it was an oversight or maybe over-confidence. I went in.

Delmonico was sitting at the same back table as he was the last time I was there, although the big guy who had been with him wasn't in the room. As my eyes adjusted, I looked around. The same two young punks who were sitting at the table on the left were still there, playing cards. That was it. A skeleton crew. No one was behind the makeshift bar or at the espresso machine. And, of course, Trullo wasn't there.

The two young guys started to stand up when I came in, putting their hands inside their jackets. Delmonico put up his hand for them to relax and they stopped in the middle of rising.

"I doubt that Mr. Shore is here to hurt me. He's probably just looking for answers to some questions. Am I correct, Mr. Shore?"

I nodded and didn't correct his formality. The two gunsel punks sat back down.

I walked over to Delmonico's table and sat down, not waiting to be invited. I wanted him to know that I was serious but relaxed. No one had searched me this time.

"Fewer guys in here than last time. Are you downsizing?"

It got a tight smile in response, but it felt like he was humoring me.

"Ah, yes. The private investigator's use of the wise-crack. Kind of a cliché, no?"

I shrugged and waited. I knew he wanted to ask questions. It didn't take long.

"I take it you're here looking for answers about Jessika? I heard she was found dead. Sad, unfortunate story, that one. But then, she lived that kind of life. Always wanting more, looking for an easy payday.

Didn't you think that, Tommy? That she enjoyed playing with fire?"

Evidently the formality had been put aside. I shook my head.

"I actually don't think that. I think she was just a naïve kid who was just trying to get by any way she could and made some mistakes with the people she trusted. It happens. What's that old saying about youth being wasted on the young?"

He snorted as he laughed. Then his face changed, and his stare turned cold.

"Do you have my property, Mr. Shore? Did she entrust it to you or tell you where it is? If so, I need you to either give it to me or find it for me. It's simple. After that, I give you my word that the whole matter is over. No retaliation, nobody else gets hurt, nothing. Not the Irishman or his sister. You go about your business, and I go about mine."

There was no modulation in his voice. Cold, hard facts. I didn't believe it for a second.

"Anthony, your word doesn't really mean much to me. And yes, I do have your property. It's hidden away, set up so that if anything happens to me, it immediately gets sent to the authorities. Not sure what they'll do with it but I'm sure it would cause you a whole lot of hassle."

I paused to make sure I had his attention. He was listening.

"But I'm betting where it'll really hurt you is with your cronies, those other members of your so-called 'thing.' I can't believe that they would be happy if that kind of information got out to the world. It would make it ugly all around for you. I doubt you would be able to get past it."

I was bluffing but I kept my facial expression unreadable, and I could see him trying to decide how much of it was true. We were both jockeying for the upper hand. He sighed.

"What do you want, Mr. Shore?"

I exhaled softly.

"I want to know everything that happened with Jessika."

Delmonico had been leaning forward slightly in his chair, but he sat back and entwined his hands behind his head. He stared at me for what seemed like a minute, smiled broadly, then smiled and began to speak.

"Maybe I should I ask if you're wearing a wire?"

I wasn't expecting that. I shook my head and started to lift my shirt up to indicate that I wasn't. He waved it off and looked away.

"I'm joking. I don't care. It wouldn't matter. You're not going to be able to use any of this anyway."

I wasn't sure if it was a veiled threat or not, but I didn't want to interrupt him telling me the story. He began relating the events to me in a matter-of-fact tone.

"Fine. I had asked Bobby Trullo, whom you met last time you were here, to follow you and see where you went, keep an eye on you. We knew you had been to the club and to her apartment. When you made Bobby in the car, we changed our plans and I had him watch Victor. Tony Aprillo kept me apprised of everything that went on in the club and I instructed him to give you full access. After you started getting too close, I had Bobby send you a warning, which you evidently didn't heed. I'm thinking it probably cost him his life."

He paused for a second to make sure I was paying rapt attention then went on.

"Nobody was really sure how much you were in on this. We knew that Victor was behind the doll and then the cat. He was definitely involved. His relationship with Jessika wasn't a secret. And true to form, he eventually led us right to her, when Bobby grabbed her.

"I had him bring her to a place we own, a factory near the harbor. They make large machinery there, used for cutting metal. It's remote and the noise there would drown out any screaming. Of course, if it eventually came to that. My initial intention was to just scare her into telling me where the book was. That was going to be it. Well, and maybe cut her a little, as a warning. That beautiful face. She stole from me, and you must realize I couldn't tolerate that. Looks bad. But I was not going to kill her. If she told me what I wanted, we would have brought her back to her boyfriend and life would go on."

He paused again, this time for effect. My heart was racing.

"That's not to say that Victor wouldn't have to pay a price as well. We would have broken enough bones on him so that he would never entertain those kinds of thoughts again. But kill them? Not my style."

Delmonico was enjoying this. It was mostly for my benefit, but it occurred to me he was also playing to the two mutts at the table. A lesson? A warning? Pick one. I pushed him some more.

"So how did she end up dying?"

He shook his head. He was looking down at the edge of the table and mindlessly rubbing a worn spot on it, as if to erase it.

"That was truly unfortunate and an accident. I was holding her by the wrists and was trying to get her to tell me what I wanted to know. She slipped out of my grasp and fell backwards. She hit her head on the cement and it split open. She died instantly."

He sounded almost joyful as he retold the story. My anger was getting the best of me. I could feel my face get hot and was trying to decide what to do. I began asking him another question when I heard a noise and the front door swung open. I turned in my seat and saw it was Victor. He had followed me here from the park. I had been so caught up in deciding what I was going to do, I hadn't noticed him tailing me. He had a .45 in his hand.

It felt like slow-motion. The two punks at the table started to get up but Victor turned quickly and put a bullet in each one, both shots dead center into their foreheads. I turned back toward Delmonico and saw he was starting to get up, reaching toward a shelf behind him where he must have had a piece hidden. I pushed the table as hard as I could, and it caught him crotch level as he turned. He let out a scream and Victor fired at him twice. The first bullet grazed his temple and the second entered his ear and came out the back of his head. He slumped over on the table, inches from me.

Victor was still standing near the door when the big guy came out of the back room. He was wearing an apron and must have been cooking back there. He had a gun in his hand and shot Victor twice before Victor was able to use his final bullets as he went down. One caught the big guy in the throat and the other directly into his chest. He fell over and was dead before he hit the floor.

I moved over to Victor and knelt down to see where he had been hit. One bullet had caught him directly in the thigh and there was blood spurting out everywhere. The other bullet had grazed his head and he was bleeding profusely from there as well.

I called 911 and yelled for an ambulance, that there had been gunshots and that a man was down and bleeding. Before I could hang up, I could hear sirens and then heard cars screeching up in front of the building. Reilly must not have waited the hour and called the cops. I opened the front door, put my hands up and went outside. Two uniformed cops grabbed me immediately. I told them there was a gun in my jacket pocket. They threw me onto the hood of their car and cuffed me. They took the gun, my sap, the car keys and my phone and yelled at me to tell them how many more guys were inside and if there were more guns. I told him I thought everyone was down, five bodies in all but that the guy nearest the door was still alive and needed help, which I had already called for. One of the cops took out his gun and went in to take a look. The other one pushed me to the side of the squad car and held my head as he pushed me down into the back seat. His partner came back outside, and I could hear him saying it was a "bloodbath."

I looked back out of the window and to my right, where I had parked the rental car. I saw Reilly standing next to it. I leaned over sideways on the seat and used my shoe to bang on the window. The cops ignored me at first, but I kept it up until one of the cops came over and asked me what the problem was.

"Those keys that were in my jacket belong to my

buddy's car. He's right over there, standing next to it. Can you give them to him?"

He glared at me, then went to talk to his partner. I thought for a minute they were gonna give me a hard time about the car being evidence, but he turned and yelled to Reilly to ask if that was his car. Reilly nodded and the cop tossed the keys to him. I saw Reilly get in, glance towards me, start it up and drive off.

I put my head back on the seat and closed my eyes.

THIRTY-ONE

It was only a few minutes later when the ambulance arrived and the two attendants rushed in to get Victor. They brought him out, loaded him into the back, and took off. Not long after that, an unmarked car pulled up and Melillo and Egan got out. They glanced into the back seat of the squad car and I could see Melillo shaking his head. They went inside.

Egan came out a few minutes later and spoke to the two cops whose car I was in. They both nodded, then got into the car and pulled out, heading towards the police station. At the station, I was perp-walked in and taken back to the room where I had been interrogated the last time.

I sat there for a few hours. I was still cuffed, and they were cutting into my wrists. My arms and shoulders were getting sore. They had taken everything I had away from me, including money, belt and shoelaces. I had said I was pretty sure I wasn't going to hang myself before they could talk to me. The desk cop said it was standard procedure.

Egan came in first, alone. He had the same file folder with him. He sat down and didn't say anything for a few minutes, then opened the file and began going through the pages and shaking his head. When he finally spoke to me, he looked up and told me that Melillo would be in shortly, then went back to the file.

Melillo came in a few minutes later. I got the sense that he had been watching through the one-way window. It occurred to me that this was a game they liked to play but I didn't see what they expected the outcome to be. The only effect it had was that I was even more irritated than I had already been.

I looked up at Melillo and asked the first question.

"How's Victor?"

Egan got up and moved over to the other chair that was in the corner. He didn't sit, instead raising up his leg to rest his shoe on it. He never stopped looking at me. Melillo sat down in the chair facing me. He took out a yellow legal pad and a pen. I could see "Prudential" on the side of the pen. It made me smile. Melillo saw it when he looked up and spoke harshly.

"This is not a humorous situation so how about I ask the questions? Then we can see about answering yours. Start from the top and tell me what happened. Don't leave anything out."

I took in a breath, exhaled loudly and started telling them everything as I remembered it, leaving out only a few details. I had previously brought them up to the point when Jessika had been taken. This time, I skipped the Trullo part and picked up from meeting with Victor and then driving down to Delmonico's club to see if he would tell me anything. I told them about the book and about Jess and Victor's stupid plan but left out that I had located it and that I had it in my possession.

They listened to my story and then, without saying anything, walked out of the room. I laid my forehead on the table and tried to utilize the one meditation lesson I'd taken a few years back. It didn't help. I couldn't get Jessika's face out of my head. It was little comfort to me that she hadn't suffered, if Delmonico had told the truth. I was still overwhelmed with the feeling I had failed her.

A few minutes later, Melillo came back in alone and came around to my side of the table.

"Stand up."

I did as I was instructed and he unlocked the cuffs, then put his hand on my shoulder and gently pushed me down in the chair again. I rubbed my wrists and waited. He had a look on his face that was hard to read. He had the same file with him and threw it on the table, opened it, looked through it quickly, then closed it again, sighed, and looked at me.

"We just heard that Victor died on the table. The shot he took to the leg hit his femoral artery and he bled out. The shot to the head exacerbated the situation."

I closed my eyes. I wasn't so much sad as I was tired. This whole thing had gone bad quickly from the start. When I opened them, Melillo was staring at me with a look of sheer disdain.

"Tell me, Shore, what made you think you could go over there and reason with these guys? You had nothing to bargain with. Did you think that you could convince Delmonico to be a nice guy, that it was in his best interest to just let bygones be bygones? That he would just let it all slide? Are you really that stupid...or are you just not telling me everything?"

I looked at him and asked, "Am I under arrest? If I am, I need to call my lawyer."

Melillo sighed again and stood up.

"No, you can go. None of the bullets at the scene were fired from your gun. Other than being a complete imbecile, you didn't break any laws. Stop at the front desk and get your stuff. We're keeping the gun and the sap. Egan wanted to charge you for those but I'm betting you have a permit for the piece and the sap isn't worth the time to do the paperwork. But you can't have it back. You'll get the gun back when we close the case. Might be a long while. Stay around New Haven in case we have more questions."

He held the door open for me and I went past him and down the hall to get my wallet, money and phone, passing Egan on the way. I heard him mutter, "Cocky asshole" but I just kept walking. I was too tired to argue, and I wasn't sure he was wrong.

I called for an Uber, and it came in two minutes. The driver stopped at the Taft and it took everything I had to get out of the car and enter the building. Once inside my apartment, I took off my shoes, climbed into bed fully dressed, and fell into a restless sleep.

The next day, I awoke around noon. My landline phone was blinking that I had missed calls and my cellphone was buzzing that I had three messages. All from Reilly. I called him back and we decided to meet at Trinity. I showered, got dressed and walked down there.

He was sitting at the bar, his usual Guinness in front of him. I sat down and Michael came over to take my order. I asked for two pours of their most expensive Irish whiskey. He brought them over and I looked at them for a few minutes, then pushed one over to Reilly and raised mine.

"To Jessika."

We clinked glasses and downed them quickly. He knew I was hurting and kept the conversation to a minimum.

"I returned the car to the rental place. There was an extra charge I had to pay. You owe me fifty-eight dollars."

I nodded and told him I was good for it. Then ordered two more from Michael.

Reilly pushed a package towards me, wrapped up in a multitude of envelopes. I asked him if he had looked at it and he shook his head and said, "No, thanks." Plausible deniability.

Over the next hour, we had two more, after which I walked back to my apartment. I was still tired and sat down in my easy chair to maybe fall back asleep, but I couldn't stop my mind from running over everything. I was fighting off guilt and I kept thinking I had missed something, something that could have made it all come out differently. I finally decided that there was nothing that I could have done to get to the proverbial happy ending. But it would be a while before I would consider taking another case.

It would take a long time to get the taste of failure out of my system.

EPILOGUE

It had been three weeks since the shootout on Wooster Street. The *Register* had done a front-page story on it the next day but I hadn't been mentioned by name, only that a number of "suspects were being held" and that the police were chalking the entire incident up to a "gangland dispute." It was sloppy journalism but I was grateful for it.

The article had mentioned the people involved and there was a small bit of information on Victor. That he had been in the service, a former marine who had won medals for marksmanship. It explained how he had taken out Delmonico and the other three so quickly and with pinpoint accuracy.

The phrase used to describe Delmonico was that he was a "local businessman with possible ties to a New York crime syndicate." They also mentioned he owned the Catwalk. The article claimed there was already talk of shutting the place down in the near future, that the section of New Haven it was in was "ripe for gentrification." They would probably raze the building and build luxury apartments. It made sense. Much of New Haven was going in that direction. They would have to do something about the rest of the neighborhood surrounding it, though.

The article also mentioned that the police were still looking into whether the shooting was tied to the body of the man who was found in the dumpster of the McDonald's on I-95. He had been a "known member of the Wooster Street crew" but that it had taken a while to identify him because of the shape the body had been found in. I knew it was Trullo and made a mental note to touch base with Mickey and thank him. I was sure there would be a monetary cost involved.

There was no mention of Jessika, in that article or in any other. I looked in the paper every day and the only mention I saw of her was a short obituary. I didn't know if she had family in town that would have placed it but then, I really didn't know that much about her at all. I eventually thought it had been the other dancers who got some money together and paid for that and for her cremation.

I needed to get out of my head, so I went out and walked the few blocks down to Trinity. It was a beautiful day. When I got there, I was pleasantly surprised to see Jennifer from The Catwalk working behind the bar. She smiled when she saw me. I sat down and ordered a Jameson.

"Hey there you. Fancy meeting again."

I smiled back.

"Yeah, small world, small town. This is my normal hangout, this and the Owl on College. Just started?"

She nodded. "Yeah, a coupla days ago. After that craziness went down on Wooster Street, they closed the

Catwalk, saying they would get back to everyone when it opened up again. It didn't sound to me like it would be too soon, so I got this gig. I like it a lot better. I can wear this t-shirt and don't have to show off my tits to the world. And the prices are much more reasonable so that people can order more drinks. My tips come out to be about the same."

I nodded, then mentioned Jessika, saying it was sad and asking whether the other dancers had put the obit in the papers.

"Yeah, they did. Everyone in the bar contributed, even that jerk Fat Tony who ran the place. We came up with enough money for the piece in the paper and then to have her cremated. We were all sad. About Victor, too. I'm sure you know he was involved in that thing on Wooster Street. Must have gone crazy after Jess was found dead and somehow blamed it on those guys. So weird."

I nodded again. It was all I had in me.

I finished my drink and paid my tab, leaving Jennifer a good tip. Once outside, I looked up at the sun and decided it was nice enough to take a walk.

I walked down past the auxiliary railroad station, over to Olive Street and then down to Grand Avenue. I thought about stopping for food again at that great bodega, but I had no appetite of late and really wasn't hungry now.

When I turned down East Street, I could see that the neon sign for The Catwalk wasn't lit. I stopped as I got closer, stared at the place for a while, and then continued walking, towards home.

A LOOK AT BOOK THREE:

MOSAIC

Private Investigator Tommy Shore has been called to go out to Wallingford, Connecticut—a little outside of his normal jurisdiction. But Carla Vitter's brother-in-law is missing, and she's all alone to care for her niece.

Worried that he got involved with the wrong type of people, Carla is on edge. And while Tommy suspects an abusive spouse—who might also be involved in a white supremacist group—the police offer no help, and he begins to wonder if they're involved as well.

As Tommy digs deeper, he uncovers truth after hidden truth, and the investigation turns nasty—culminating in a question of whether anyone will come out unscathed.

Part noir, part throwback, part travelogue to one of the great small cities, Mosaic is book three in the Tommy Shore Mystery series.

AVAILABLE AUGUST 2022

ABOUT THE AUTHOR

Lawrence Dorfman has more than thirty years of experience in the bookselling world, including stints at Simon and Schuster, Penguin, and Harry N. Abrams. He is the author of the bestselling Snark Handbook series including *The Snark Handbook: Politics and Government Edition*, *The Snark Handbook: Insult Edition*; *The Snark Handbook: Sex Edition*, *Snark! The Herald Angels Sing*, and *The Snark Handbook: Clichés Edition*. He lives in Hamden, CT with his wife.

Made in the USA
Columbia, SC
29 November 2022

72248479R00114